Nightmare Town

Nightmare Town

by T. ERNESTO BETHANCOURT

Holiday House · New York

Library of Congress Cataloging in Publication Data

Bethancourt, T   Ernesto.
  Nightmare town.

  SUMMARY: The residents of Celestial, Arizona and
the object of their strange religion are unlike
anyone or anything a 16-year-old have ever encountered.
  [1. Science fiction]   I. Title.
PZ7.B46627Ni   [Fic]   79-2091
ISBN 0-8234-0366-1

For John Briggs

Contents

Nightmare Town

1 · Good Old Uncle Andy

It was on account of my dad that my troubles began. Or if you want to think about it the other way, on account of my mom. She got sick when I was thirteen. Cancer. Up to then, we were real happy together, my mom, Dad, and me. Not that we was rich or anything. My dad worked for Amalgamated Copper in Long Island City. Which isn't part of Long Island at all. It's part of Queens, one of the five boroughs of New York City. We used to live in Astoria, about five miles from Dad's job.

Dad got laid off at Amalgamated just a month or two before Mom got sick. Being between jobs so long, his Blue Cross had expired. And there was Dad, looking at all those extra bills from the hospital piling up like crazy. He didn't want to worry Mom, so each time he seen her at the hospital, he told her he was back to work.

But we were really in a bad way for coins. That's when Dad took a chance and lost. He decided he was gonna be some kind of Jesse James and hold up a liquor store. Dad had a gun. So did the clerk at the liquor store. When all the smoke cleared away, the clerk was dead, and my dad was doing twenty years to life for felony murder at a prison upstate. Mom died two weeks after the stick-up. She never even knew.

I don't know what woulda happened if my Uncle Andy and Aunt Catherine hadn't taken me in. I guess the court woulda put me in a foster home. Tell you true, I wish they would of. My Uncle Andy is the biggest stiff that ever marched in a Veteran's Day parade. Yeah, he does that every year. Funny suit, tin hat, and all.

And Uncle Andy's always running his mouth about how the commies are gonna take over if we ain't careful. I don't think he ever saw a commie in his life, but he's sure they're everywhere. Like, if he gets trouble at the job, or at a store, anybody who does him wrong is a commie. When you consider that my uncle has a personality like a subway men's room, the whole world is out to get him. And that makes them all commies so far as he's concerned.

Uncle Andy is my dad's older brother. He hated my dad since they was both kids. Maybe it's because my dad is one good-looking dude, and Uncle Andy . . . well, his looks fit his personality. I understand that my grandmother always loved my dad more than Uncle Andy, and it ate on him real bad. And because I look just like my dad, I guess it gave Uncle Andy a chance to get back at him through me. From the pictures I've seen in the family album Aunt Catherine keeps, I look just like my dad did back then.

Say, I don't know how to put this without sounding like some kind of ego monster. So screw it, I'll say it. I happen to be a very good-looking dude. No crap. I been hearing it all my life. When my folks was still together, everybody always was telling them I was a beautiful child, if you're ready for that. And I stayed with it, too.

I'm a little over six feet tall, weigh a hundred and seventy-five pounds, and I never had a pimple in my life. I got dark, wavy hair and blue eyes. Some of the chicks at Astoria High, where I used to go, say I look like John Travolta. I don't think so, but when a chick thinks that, you're a dummy to tell her different. I make out okay. But I never hooked up steady with any one chick.

I tell you, it's one funny feeling. I had chicks tell me how much they cared, but nothing came back from inside me. Maybe they was just hung up on the way I look, because they didn't seem to care there was no feelings on my side.

Uncle Andy's about five-ten, nearly two hundred pounds, and getting bald. Fast. He had bad skin when he was a kid, too. Even today, he's got a complexion like a golf ball with scars. I heard it said that beauty is only skin deep. Well, my uncle is ugly right down to his bones. He is one mean mother, my uncle.

My Aunt Catherine is a nice lady. But after all the years with my Uncle Andy, she's kinda whipped. Like she gave up on fighting life, or Uncle Andy. He's a dictator in his house. When he comes home, dinner is on the table or else. If it ain't hot enough, no matter when he gets in, he makes Aunt Catherine do it all over again. And he's forever talking out of the Bible. Anything happens, he got a quote. All by himself, Uncle Andy is hard to take. But it isn't just him. There's my cousins, Jackie and Irene.

Jackie and Irene are little, ugly copies of my uncle. To give you an idea of where they're at, for the four years I lived with them, they put me down. You'll love the reason: I'm the son of a murderer! Now, I ask you, what did I have to do with what my dad did? In fact, I only really found out what Dad did when I was sixteen, last year. Up to then, Uncle Andy told me that my dad was dead.

The way I found out, I came across a letter to me from Dad. He'd been writing to me while I'd been at Uncle Andy's, and Uncle Andy had been throwing the letters away. I started in writing to Dad after that on the quiet, since I can't go see him until I'm eighteen.

When I wrote to Dad, I didn't tell him that Uncle Andy and his family been crapping on me. I figure he's got enough to worry about, being up there. But he should be up for parole in another five years. He says in his letters that when he gets out, we're going to be together again. But in the meantime, I had to deal with his brother by myself. And his brother's kids. I can't bring myself to call them my cousins.

They're a coupla years older than me. So being that much hipper, they decided they were going to stick it to me for what my dad done. They were even nice enough to fill in all the kids at my new school about my old man. First time I came home from school crying about it, and told my Aunt Catherine, all I got was a sermon. Something about the sins of the fathers being visited on the sons. Aunt Catherine told me I should be a good Christian and turn the other cheek. Easy for her to say. She wasn't getting all the crap I was.

That's when my reputation as a fighter and a troublemaker got started at Astoria High. See, I knew I couldn't hit on Jackie or Irene for doing it. First time I tried, Uncle Andy gave me such a going over that I couldn't go to school for two days. But nobody said I couldn't let the other kids at school have it for mouthing off about my old man.

I used to get beat up regular. Then I started working out in the school gym and at the Youth Center. By the time I was fifteen, I was the size I am now and wasn't taking any crap from anyone. The kids at school left me alone after I bent a few of them real good. But I still couldn't do anything about Jackie and Irene. And they knew it and rubbed it in every chance they got.

I put up with it for four years. All I had going for me was that I sneaked a copy of Uncle Andy's mailbox key and traded letters with my father. The mailman comes in my neighborhood at about ten-thirty in the morning, after Uncle Andy's gone to work. My dad's letters come regular as clockwork on Tuesdays and Fridays. I used to wait and pick them up. It made me late for school twice a week, but what did I care? Besides, any letters from the school to Uncle Andy, I could get to before he did. I used to write my own excuse letters to school. Signed Uncle Andy's name, too.

But writing my own excuse letters is what brought the whole mess to a head. See, I never had a place to study or get my homework done at Uncle Andy's house. Soon as he was home, he was at me about one thing or another. After a while, I just said screw the school work. I got myself a part-time job at Food King Market, delivering groceries and, more often than not, I'd take in a flick instead of going to school. Finally, the school sent a letter saying that if I didn't shape up, I wasn't gonna graduate.

The letter came on a Saturday, when Uncle Andy was home. I didn't know anything about it coming. I was taking in a kung-fu flick at the Loew's Astoria. I stopped off to grab a burger at the White Castle so I wouldn't have to look at my "family" at dinner time. I didn't get back until about eight-thirty that night.

Uncle Andy was waiting for me when I come in the door. I wasn't two steps inside the house when he lays a sucker punch on me. And he don't hit with no open hand. He punches. Hard.

When he slammed me on the side of the head, I guess

I nutted out. Maybe it was the kung-fu flick I just come from. Anyway, before he could hit me again, I rapped him a coupla good ones, bladehand like Bruce Lee. He falls backwards and hits his head on the coffee table in front of the living-room couch. Soon as he hits the deck, he rolls over and lies real still.

Jackie and Irene was there. They knew I was gonna get it from my uncle, and they wouldna missed the show for the world. Jackie takes one look at his old man laid out and hollers, "Murderer! You killed my dad! You're a killer, just like your father. I'm calling the cops!"

I guess that four solid years of being crapped on by the whole family came to the surface. I just didn't care anymore. When my cousin went toward the phone, I grabbed his arm and spun him around. Then I let him have my best right. Straight on the end of his pimply nose. I felt it squish under my knuckles, and it was just fine. Jackie started to bleed from the nose like crazy.

Soon as she sees the blood, my cousin Irene lets out a scream you could of heard in Brooklyn. Aunt Catherine comes running in from the kitchen. She always hides there so she don't see me getting knocked around by Uncle Andy. She takes one look at my uncle on the floor, Jackie bleeding like a stuck pig, and Irene screaming. Then she passes out cold.

I knew that I really did it this time. So I pulled out the phone. I knew there was still the extension in the upstairs bedroom, but I didn't want anyone calling the cops just then. See, I made up my mind that I was going to split this pop stand. But I sure didn't want to have the room next door to my old man in prison. That meant I had to get far, far away from Astoria.

I only had a few bucks in my pocket. I walked into the kitchen and emptied out my Aunt Catherine's sugar bowl. I felt bad about it, too. It was the money she had saved for I don't know how long. Uncle Andy handles all the money in the house and gives her an allowance, like she was a kid instead of a grown woman. There was almost sixty bucks in the sugar bowl. I would have gone back and emptied out Uncle Andy's wallet, too. But I didn't hear Irene anymore. That meant she had to be upstairs calling the cops. There wasn't time to pack a bag. I ran out the kitchen door in what I was wearing: T-shirt, jeans, sneakers, and my leather jacket.

It was only five blocks to the subway from my uncle's house, and I ran all the way. In a few minutes, I was headed for Manhattan. It wasn't until I was on the train that I realized I didn't have idea one about where I was gonna go. I sure wasn't gonna stick around New York. For all I knew, Uncle Andy was dead as a mackerel. It was then I decided to go to Hollywood.

I figured that all these years people been telling me I'm good looking. Might as well have a shot at getting into TV and movies. I was kinda sketchy on where Hollywood was from Astoria. I knew it was south and west of New York. So I changed trains at Times Square and, in fifteen minutes, I was standing at the Holland

Tunnel entrance off Canal Street in downtown Manhattan. I got a ride pretty quick as far as the entrance to the New Jersey Turnpike.

After an hour or so, this truck rolls up. It was a big, tractor-trailer job. The driver opened the door and waved me in.

"Where you headed?" he asked.

"California," I said.

"Well, I'm goin' to Cleveland," says the driver.

"Close enough," I say, climbing into the cab.

The driver worked the gears, and we pulled away from the toll plaza. Once we swung onto the highway, the truck picked up speed. I looked back over my shoulder. I could still see the New York skyline, all lit up and shiny. In front of us, the road began to unwind. Pretty soon, there was no light but the big splash of the truck's headlights ahead. I all of a sudden realized I was on my way. I didn't know how or if I was gonna make it, but I was sure on my way!

2 · On the Road

"So you goin' to California, huh?" asked the driver. I looked over at him and, even though the light was dim in the cab of the truck, I could see him good. I guess my eyes had gotten used to the dark by then. He was a little, red-faced guy. I'd say he was in his forties. Real old anyway. It looked like he didn't shave but once a week. And tomorrow was the day. He had a plaid shirt and jeans on, and he was wearing an Atlanta Braves baseball cap. He was still looking at me, waiting for an answer.

"Yeah."

"Well, ain't you just the talky little devil," the driver said. "Looka here. I picked you up to keep me company, boy. I got to get this bleeping sonofa bleeping bleep to Cleveland by eight o'bleeping clock tomorrow morning. I been partyin' since six o'bleeping clock this morning. I feel like a cow pat that's been rained on. And if you don't keep me awake, I'm dam' near liable to pile this bleeping truck all over the mother bleeping state of New bleeping Jersey."

I think you get the idea that this driver didn't teach Sunday school on his off days. I mean, I heard some salty talkers before, but this driver was something else. I think he coulda got bleep into the Lord's Prayer, somewhere. So I'm just gonna tell you what he said, not the way he said it. Almost.

"Geez, I'm sorry," I said. "I'm kinda tired, myself."

"Big day, huh, kid?"

"Sure was," I said. "I can't take too many more of these."

"I know how y'feel, boy," said the driver. "Tell y'what. Ol' Doctor Skaggs got what's good for you." He reached over and took a tin box marked FIRST AID from behind the seat, where the bed is on those big trucks. He fumbled around and came up with a tiny bottle of whiskey, like you see in the liquor stores. Then he handed me a pill bottle.

"Open 'er up, will you?" he said. "These new kid-proof caps, y'need two hands." I opened the bottle and saw what was inside. Looked like diet pills, with little green grains inside the capsules. Aunt Catherine used to take them. I wondered how many he wanted. I found out. He put the opened bottle to his lips. For a crazy minute there, I thought he was gonna swallow the whole bottle, like they was M & M's. But he was smooth. He snaked two caps out of the bottle with the end of his tongue. Then he washed the pills down with a shot from the miniature bottle of whiskey.

"Help y'self, boy," the driver said. "I got plenty. But they ain't no more whiskey. You're gone to have to eat them raw."

"What are they?" I asked. Not because I would of taken one, but because I was kinda scared. If this driver got all doped up, he was liable to get us both killed.

"Am-phet-a-MINE," said the driver. "Never leave home without it. Keeps you bright-eyed and bushy-tailed. Specially on a long haul like this. For us independents, it's the only way to fly."

"Excuse me, but what's an independent?" I asked. I never heard that expression for a speed freak before.

"Independent trucker, boy," he said. "This here's my rig. I don't work for no company, nor no man in the world. I'm what you call a en-try-prah-noor. I don't even belong to no trucker's association or what have you. I'm a born non-joiner. Only mistake I ever made was joinin' things. Joined the Army in 1949 when it was all peaceful. Then the Korean War happened. That done it for me. I ain't joined a thing since. Not unless you want to count me almost marryin' Laura Sue Ciphers down home. I managed to get out of that, too." He laughed until he coughed.

I was thinking to myself that if this dude picked me up for company, maybe I should say something once in a while. But I guess his idea of company was an audience. He kept up a running chatter until we were halfway through Pennsylvania.

I found out that his name was Arnie Skaggs. That he

came from Macon, Georgia. That he owned his own truck and went where his work was. That he figured he musta traveled around the whole world a coupla hundred times, just in the miles he put on the truck. In fact, I heard so much of Arnie Skaggs, I was starting to fall out. I didn't think he would of noticed, either. He was into a speed rap. I coulda been a statue. It wouldna mattered to him.

But just the other side of Harrisburg, Pennsylvania, he said to me, "But, boy, you never told me why you're goin' to California. Come to think of it, I don't even know your name."

"Jimmy. Jimmy Hunter."

"Good name. Now, what's takin' you out to California, boy?"

"My dad's out there," I lied. "He and my mom been separated. I been living with her. But now he says he's all set out there. So I'm going out to live with him."

"He can't be too set, son," said Arnie Skaggs, "if he couldn't send you at least a bus ticket."

"Whadda you mean?" I said, and I don't know why I did, "he's set up just great. He's a . . . vice president with Amalgamated Copper out there. He wanted to send me a plane ticket. But I didn't wanna take it. I wanna see the country, that's all."

"Okay, soldier, okay," said Arnie Skaggs. "Myself, I don't care if you some millionaire playboy who's hitchin' just for a laugh. In fact, I don't care if you're the Lone Ranger or Jack the Ripper. Just long as you're good company to Cleveland."

Arnie Skaggs shut up for almost fifteen minutes. I was on the edge of falling out when he said, "Looka, boy. I know you're on the run. And, like I say, I don't care what you done. Less you some kind of pervert. You ain't that, are you?"

"No."

"But you are on the run, ain't you?"

"Yeah," I admitted.

"Cops or family?" he asked.

"Both," I said. "But not real family. I mean, my dad's brother. I used to live with him."

Before I knew what was happening, I had told the whole tale to Arnie Skaggs. I don't know why. And I didn't leave anything out. I didn't try to make myself look better or worse. When I was done, Arnie said, "Was you uncle dead or just out cold, son?"

"I don't know," I replied, leveling with him. "Maybe he was dead. But I'll tell you this. If he was, I don't care. I mean, I wouldn't ever wanna kill anyone on purpose. But if he is dead, I'm sorry. I just don't care."

"Can't say as I blame you, Jimmy," said Arnie Skaggs. "It seems to me that your uncle is one bad man. But you could be in deep trouble. Or mebbe just in a little. Ain't no tellin'."

We drove in silence for a while, then Arnie slapped his forehead and said, "What's the matter with me? You can find out for yourself. Looka here. Next stop we make, you get on the telephone. You make a person-to-person call to your mean uncle. If he comes to the phone, he sure ain't dead."

He was right, of course. Then I had another idea.

"But won't they know where I am? I mean, trace the call?" I asked.

"What you think you are, some desperado, Jimmy?" laughed Skaggs. "If you really did your uncle in, chances are the cops are lookin' for you in New York. They prolly expect you to be hidin' around the backyard someplace." Skaggs laughed. "Besides, you gonna be callin' from a pay phone. Takes time to trace a call. And you sure don't want to stay on the line and jaw with your uncle, do you?"

"No, and that's for sure," I said.

"Well, there you go, then." Arnie Skaggs began playing a tune on the big truck's gear box. Slowing down. "There's a phone a mile or two down the road. All by itself on the road. Whup! Here 'tis!"

We almost missed the phone booth by the roadside, but Skaggs managed to stop the big truck in time.

"You got a lotta change, boy?" he asked. I hadn't thought of it. I never called anyone long distance. I forgot here I was, a lot further away from New York than I ever been in my life. I kept thinking it was a ten-cent call. I checked my pockets and found about forty cents in loose change. I told Skaggs how much I had.

"Almost enough, Jimmy," he said, digging into his pocket. "Yeah, I got over a buck here." He handed me five quarters. I finally got an operator on the line and got the call put through. The phone rang five times, then I heard my Aunt Catherine pick up.

"Mr. Andrew Hunter, please," said the operator. "Long Distance calling."

"Just a minute," said my aunt.

"In a short time, I heard this sleepy voice come on the line.

"Hullo? . . . Hullo?" said my uncle. It was all I wanted to know. I hung up the phone and sprinted back to the truck. As I climbed into the cab, I said to Skaggs, "He's alive." Skaggs grinned and put the truck in gear.

"Mixed emotions, huh, Jimmy?" he said. "Glad you ain't no killer, but sorry your bad-ass uncle's still around. Kinda like seein' your worst enemy total your new Cadillac. You don't know whether to laugh or cry."

That one didn't need an answer. We rode on in silence for a few miles. Then Arnie Skaggs asked, "What you figger you gone do in California, Jimmy?"

"I dunno. I thougnt I'd have a shot at getting in movies or maybe TV. If I can."

"Well, you a good-lookin' kid, Jimmy. Mebbe you can. I been to California. It's real pretty country. But I don't know nothin' about the movie business. 'Cept I like Burt Reynolds' movies. You see that one where he totals Jackie Gleason's whole fleet of POH-leece cars? Drivin' a box-load of beer? I laughed so hard at that one. Reminds me of the time I was runnin' to Tampa from Atlanta back in '69. I was comin' past Valdosta, when this Smokey come up . . ."

In a few minutes, Skaggs was telling me this whole long tale about him and some Georgia cop. I think I fell out in the middle of it. Next thing I know, I feel Skaggs shaking my shoulder.

"Rise and shine, Jimmy," he said. "Grab your socks. It's stone-bone daylight outside. There's my turnoff for Cleveland comin' up. You want to get yourself another ride, this here's the spot."

Skaggs brought the big truck to a stop. I opened the door and said, "Thanks a lot, Arnie. I appreciate what you did."

"Nothin' to it, Jimmy," he said, waving a hand. "Lissen. You okay for money? I mean, I could spare a few bucks, if you between a rock and a hard place."

"Nah," I said. "I'm okay. But thanks just the same." See, I didn't tell him about the sugar bowl I emptied out in Aunt Catherine's kitchen. I mean, it didn't have nothing to do with why I was on the run. It was just kinda extra.

"All right, boy," hollered Skaggs from the cab as he started up the truck again. "Good talkin' with y'all!" In a few minutes, all I could see of the truck was the plume of diesel smoke from the big straight pipe that poked into the air above the cab.

I only waited about a half hour before I seen the next car. It was a new Chevy Malibu Classic with a man driving. At first, I didn't think he was gonna stop. He slowed down, like he was looking me over, then went about a hundred yards past me. But then he stopped and honked his horn. I ran down the road and got in.

The driver of the car was this guy about fifty years old. He was wearing a shirt and tie, and he had a suit coat on a hanger in the back of the four-door Chevy. He had lotsa stuff in the back, all packed up in boxes. He must of seen me looking at them.

"Samples," he says. "Shoes. All left shoes. Don't carry a full pair anywhere. That way, they ain't worth stealing. I sell ladies shoes. Name's Ben Holtz. From St. Louis. I'm on my way home. What's your name, son?"

"Hunter. Jimmy Hunter."

"Are you going far?" he says.

"California," I said. Then I started looking around the car. See, I smelled something. I figured at first that maybe Holtz ran over an animal on the road, and the dead smell was coming in through the air vents.

"Well, I'm going as far as St. Louis," says Ben Holtz, like he didn't smell nothing. "I can give you a lift that far. I'd be glad for the company. It gets very lonely on the road for weeks at a time."

As he ran on, it dawned on me. Holtz hadn't run over no skunk. The smell I was getting was pure Ben Holtz! And with all the windows in the Chevy run up, it was strong enough inside the car to chew the air. Either this guy never heard of pit spray or his nose was numb. Ain't any wonder the guy was lonely. With a smell like that, he'd always get a seat in the subway. With a coupla seats on each side!

"I really miss my family," says Ben Holtz. "I've been a salesman all my life. It was different when I was single. But now, with my family . . . Say, would you like to see a picture?" Ben Holtz reached into his hip pocket to get his wallet. I wanted to retch. Each time he moved around, I got a new wave of pure locker room. I took the picture he showed me. A fat lady with two kids, both boys. I wondered if they noticed how bad Holtz smelled. Probably not.

"Nice," I said, handing him back the picture.

"Of course, they're much older now. Allen, my oldest son, is married. Made me a grandfather last spring," said Ben Holtz proudly.

I couldn't take it any more. I opened the window on my side, just a crack, to get some air circulating. Holtz noticed and said, "A little warm?"

"Yeah," I said.

"Well, don't worry," says Holtz. "I have air-conditioning. We can have all the fresh air you want." He pushed a button on the dashboard and, in a while, the car cooled off. I couldn't help wondering how this guy made out as a salesman. Man, if anybody that rank got close to me, I'd want to get away.

But for all of smelling bad, Holtz was an all-right guy. And he didn't seem to notice that I stayed way over on the other side of the front seat. He ran on telling me about his territory, and how sales weren't what they used to be. Chain shoe stores were hurting his business, he said. Cut-rate this, cut-rate that. Said that only his old-time customers were keeping him in business anymore.

I didn't want to say that if he wasn't strong as a day-old mackerel, he might do better. But I listened on as the road unwound in front of us. After a while, I actually started to like this pitty dude. I mean, he had a good heart. He was putting his last son through college, and it was rough going. But he was one of these guys who wave their arms when he talked. And each time he did, it wasn't so much the smell as the way it burned your eyes!

We stopped for lunch in Indianapolis. Ben wanted to buy lunch for me. Right then and there, I figured I'd do the guy a solid.

"Ben," I says. "You been telling me how your only good customers left are the old-timers you been selling to for years, right?"

"Right. I don't know how to talk to young folks, it seems."

"Maybe that ain't it Ben," I says. "Young people are into cologne and smelling good. Haven't you noticed?"

"Have I?" says Holtz, leaning across the table. I couldn't help it; I leaned back. "Sissified, I call it! Like these barbershops with lady barbers and hairnets, blow dryers. Why a man should smell like a man!"

I put my foot in it then. I said, "Yeah, Ben. But not like a goat. Mebbe you should clean up your act. I mean, I been riding with you for over two hundred miles in a closed car. Now, I don't want to give you no offense but honest, Ben, a little cologne wouldn't hurt."

Ben Holtz gives me a look like his dog just died. I knew I'd hurt his feelings. I could of bit off my tongue. See, I didn't want to make him feel bad. I wanted to help him out for being nice to me.

Holtz fiddled with his coffee cup for a few seconds, then says, "I guess you're right, Jim. I never gave it much thought. I just know that I carry the best line of ladies shoes in the territory. And my prices are fair for the quality I deliver. Nowadays, maybe that's not enough . . . I don't know." He stood up. "But this isn't getting me home," he said a bit cooly. "It's a long way to St. Louis."

I got up, too, and we split the check at the cashier's counter. Holtz told me he hadda gas up. I told him I'd meet him at the gas pumps. I went to the men's room. With all this talk about smelling gamy, I wasn't too sure I smelled like any rose, either. I figured a little clean-up wouldn't hurt.

In the washroom, I checked myself out in the mirror. I didn't look too good. I shave twice a week, and when I split from Uncle Andy's was the day I was due. My clothes looked like I slept in them. Come to think of it, I had. Just for a few hours in Arnie Skagg's truck. All the talk about grooming made me feel like an armpit.

They had these coin machines in the john. You maybe saw them before. They sell little trick puzzles, toys, first-aid kits, y'know? In one of the slots for two quarters, you could buy a throwaway razor. I pushed in the coins, and I shaved. I hadda use that crappy green liquid soap that they got in those dispensers. It hurt my face, and I felt like a public washroom, the way the soap smelled. But I was clean shaven.

When I came out of the john, I looked around, and no Ben Holtz. I went outside, and the car wasn't where he parked it. I figured I musta hurt his feelings. Maybe I couldn't blame him for taking off. Then I spotted his car. He was over at the gas pumps, filling up. I began running toward him, waving. He was just paying off the gas pump jockey. I wanted to tell him I was sorry I hurt his feelings.

He sees me, and gives me a wave, like good-bye. I start in running then, because no matter how he smelled, this dude was a lift to St. Louis. But he never slowed down. I hollered a "wait up" but he was rolling by then. I guess I wasn't watching where I was running. I just didn't want to be left behind. I ran right in front of this Mercedes Benz sedan that was pulling up to the gas pumps. It knocked me ass over head. And the next thing I know, I'm sitting on the ground in front of the car. This well-dressed dude about forty years old is looking into my face and saying, "Are you all right, son?"

3 · The Gaynors

"Sure, sure," I said. "I'm okay. My fault anyhow. I was trying to get my lift before he left."

"Well, I'm taking you to a hospital, young fella," says the well-dressed dude. "You may have injuries you don't know about."

That'd be all I need, I thought. They get me to some hospital, I'll have to make out forms, show I.D. and all. I'd be in a juvenile slam inside of twenty-four hours. But the guy gave me an idea.

"Look," I said. "I'm all right. Really I am. You want to do me a favor, you can give me a lift. I just missed my ride. That way, if I ain't okay, you'll know. I'd be right with you in the car. If you got the room, that is."

I looked over at the car. There was a lady in the front seat and a real pretty girl, about my age, in back. They had their faces pressed to the windows to see what was going on with me. The guy hesitated, like he was thinking it over. I had a chance to check him out.

He was wearing one of those shirts that's got an

alligator instead of a pocket on it, real sharp slacks, and a pair of boots I knew cost a pile of coin. He was fair-haired and blue-eyed with a slim build. He was also worried, I could tell. Like he wasn't too hot on the idea of picking up a hitchhiker. But he didn't know I was in trouble, so I kinda had him by the curlies. From the luggage rack on the car and the Ohio tags I spotted, they were a family on vacation. If he took me to a hospital or something, he would of been tied up with cops and insurance forms forever. And lost all the time off his vacation. I could almost hear the gears in his head turning. He finally made up his mind.

"Okay," he says, "hop in back."

I did, before he had a chance to think about it any more.

"Where you headed?" asks the guy driving.

"California," I said.

"Really?" says the girl next to me. "What part? We're on our way to Los Angeles."

Before I could answer, the guy driving says, "A long hitchhike without any suitcase, isn't it?"

"I had a kit," I lied, "but my lift took off with it in his car. I guess he forgot it was there. That's why I was running after him." The driver nodded his head. "And ain't it great?" I said. "I'm going to L.A., too."

"Some luck," says the driver. And I knew he wasn't talking about my luck. He knew he was stuck. But I didn't care. I wasn't hurt, and I got myself a free ride in a Mercedes Benz all the way to Los Angeles!

"That's quite a long haul to hitchhike, isn't it?" asks the lady in the front seat.

"I want to see the country," I lied. "I never been west of New Jersey before. I'm from New York."

"We're from Cleveland," says the chick next to me. "Have you ever been to Los Angeles?"

"Nah," I said. "Just New York, like I toldja."

"Oh, yes," she says. "That's what you just said, isn't it? What's you name? My name is Liz. Liz Gaynor. That's my mom and dad."

"Jimmy. Jimmy Hunter. Pleasetameetcha," I said.

"I'm Bill Gaynor," said the driver, "and this is my wife, Ellen."

I told them I was glad to meet them.

"Do you have family in California, Jimmy?" asks Ellen Gaynor.

"Nah. I ain't got family nowhere," I lied again. "I'm a orphan. I just turned eighteen and got out of St. Joseph's Home for Boys in Queens. Now I'm on my own, I figured I never seen the country or California, so I just picked up and split."

I don't know if Bill Gaynor bought the story or not. He only said, "I see." I caught the look between him and his wife, though. I made a note to myself that as soon as we made the next stop, I was gonna split. I mean, I knew that Uncle Andy was alive, but I was still on the run. All I needed was for this rich guy to blow the whistle on me. Before you know it, I'd be in a cop car, headed back to New York and a reform school.

But the rich guy didn't hang on the subject. He and his wife started talking quiet in the front seat. I don't know about what. I couldn't hear on accounta Liz Gaynor was some rap artist.

Inside of a half hour, she lets me know that she's seventeen years old, a senior in high school, and that she's gonna go to college next year. That she wants to study drama and maybe be an actress. Now, when she says this, my ears pick up. I didn't even know you could study how to be an actor in no college. I always thought college was for learning how to be a doctor or a lawyer or something like that.

I was all set to tell her how I wanted to maybe get into the movies or on TV, but I clammed up. I hadda be careful, y'see. I figure if the cops really start looking for me, it wouldn't do to be telling everyone I meet all about myself. In fact, I was kinda sorry I gave my real name. But what name would I of given? So while she ran on, I kinda listened with one ear while I started in thinking of a new name for myself.

I never cared too much for the name Jimmy. But it happened that way. My dad is James Hunter, and I'm James Hunter, Jr. To be able to call us without confusion, my mom called my dad Jim and me Jimmy. And Jimmy I been ever since.

I always liked James Garner in movies and on TV. I was thinking of maybe calling myself Jim something. Like Rockford, the way Garner does on TV. I was going through Rockwell and names with rock in them.

Then I thought, Stone. Jim Stone. It sounds like the kinda name a movie star should have. I figured the next time somebody asks me, I'm Jim Stone.

And just like she was reading my mind, Liz Gaynor says to me, "But when I'm an actress, I'm going to change my name. I mean, Liz Gaynor. Who'd believe that name? It makes you think I was stealing Liz Taylor's name. It's so close, don't you think?"

I guess Liz's mother heard what was going down in the back seat.

"You were named for your grandmother, darling. And there's no reason for you to change your name. Liz or Elizabeth Gaynor is a fine name."

"But that's not Daddy's real name, either," protested Liz. "He told me how he picked out Gaynor for his name."

I did a take. What was with these people? They tell me their name is one thing, now their daughter tells me it ain't their name at all. I guess Ellen Gaynor seen the look on my face, on accounta she says, "Don't be confused, Jimmy. My husband is like you. He was an orphan. He was raised in an orphanage outside of Cleveland, right, dear?"

"Right, dear," says Bill Gaynor and goes back to driving.

"And his favorite teacher at the orphanage was a man named Reverend Gaynor. When Bill was left on a doorstep at the orphanage, he had a note pinned to his blanket that said his name was William. He picked the

name Gaynor because of his respect for Reverend
Gaynor. Isn't that right, dear?"

"Right, dear," said Gaynor. I was beginning to see
where Liz got her talky ways from. Her mom was a
nonstop rap artist, too.

"And it was Reverend Gaynor that helped Bill get
his scholarship to Ohio State. And Bill did the rest.
With hard work, he made himself into an architect."

"I think the state university system and GI Bill from
Korea helped a little, dear," said Gaynor, speaking for
the first time in miles.

"And we met in college," said Ellen Gaynor, not
even letting on that Bill Gaynor said a word. "And it all
happened because of Reverend Gaynor. So don't you
see, Liz? Gaynor is a fine name for two fine men. Your
daddy and the Reverend Gaynor. As to the Elizabeth
part, there have been Elizabeths well before Elizabeth
Taylor. The Queen of England, for one. Or are you
forgetting her?"

"Oh, Mommy," says Liz, like she was saying what a
drag.

I don't know what woulda been said from there but,
just then, Bill Gaynor started slowing down the Mercedes, and we pulled up at a roadside restaurant and
motel.

It wasn't no cheapo-sleazo joint, either. Not a
Ho-Jo's or a chain. It had this big sign that said HARE
AND HOUNDS INNE.

Big, thick red rugs on the floor, stained glass all

around, and old-fashioned lamps. Everyone was dressed so great. Just like the Gaynors all was. I felt like a piece of trash just being there. And I betcha if I hadna been with the Gaynors, that's just what I woulda been treated like.

This waiter dude comes up and gives me a frosty look, then once he sees the Gaynors behind me, he's all smiles and polite. That's what a little cash'll do for you every time, pal. The waiter brings us to this real fancy table and gives us menus, just like on TV or the movies. Real big menus with half the stuff written in French, yet. And that ain't all of it. I take a look at the prices, and I nearly dropped my teeth! I mean, a club sandwich was the cheapest thing I seen on the menu and, at that price, I coulda eaten for a few days at McDonald's.

The waiter asks Gaynor if he wants a drink before dinner. And he looks at me, too. Now, I usedta have a beer or two with the guys I hung with in Astoria. One of them had a phony I.D., and he usedta get a six-pack at the deli. But I ain't much on drinking. Don't like the taste, same as smoking. I ain't no goody-goody or some kinda turkey, I wancha to know. I just never seen the sense in laying out coins for something I don't like, you dig?

So Gaynor orders himself a martini, and Mrs. Gaynor asks for a glass of wine. Then her and Liz get up from the table to go freshen up in the ladies room. I thought at first Gaynor was going too. On account of when Liz and her mom got up, so did he. Realizing he was just showing good manners, I stood up, too. Once Ellen and Liz had gone, we sat there looking at each other. Then Gaynor says, "Look, Jimmy, if that really is your name, I want you to know you're not fooling me for a second. No, don't protest your innocence. You're a runaway. And if you're eighteen, I'm Raquel Welch. Frankly, you look like trouble to me. But my wife thought you were a clean-looking kid, and my daughter is a romantic sort. She thinks you look like John Travolta. For some perverse reason, probably because of your orphan tale, I thought I'd give you a decent meal. But after this meal, I want you to beg off. I want you to go your own way. We'll be taking a room here at the Inn. If you don't have the money to stay here, I'll even pick up the bill."

"I got money of my own," I said. "I pay for where I go, and I don't need no handout from some rich stiff who thinks he's some kinda god because he got coins. And I ain't gonna sit here and take no crap from you. Maybe I ain't no big money man. But your old lady and your daughter ain't gonna get no disease from me. And to tell you the truth, I can't afford this joint. I'm splitting right now. I got places to go."

I started to get up but, just then, I spot Liz and her mother coming back. Gaynor sees them, too.

"Sit down, Jimmy," he says. "I'm sorry. I know what being broke is like. Perhaps I've forgotten. At least have the meal, by way of apology. We'll talk more later."

I was gonna tell him to sit on it. But by then, Liz and her mother were at the table. I sat down. And when the waiter came by, I ordered a big steak, too. If this Gaynor guy wants to be a big shot, let him pay, I figure. After that, I got busy. I never had a meal where you got all those forks and spoons. I didn't know which one you used for what. So what I did was watch what everybody else did and did the same.

Man, that meal was something else! I even found out that *filet mignon* is a little steak. When I seen it on the menu, I thought it was some kinda Chinese dish. You know, like Moo Goo Gai Pan? I thought it was Fi-Let Mig-Non. Yeah, go ahead and laugh, if you wanna. I mean, I just didn't know is all.

I was glad I didn't have to talk any more to Bill Gaynor. I was still burning from his cheap shot at me. But even if I'da wanted to talk, it wouldna mattered. On accounta Ellen Gaynor started in rapping and, when she wasn't at it, Liz was. We finished the meal and went to the desk, where the rooms got rented. Gaynor got a room for him and his wife and separate rooms for me and Liz. When we was going up the stairs, he turns to me and says, so Liz and his wife can't hear, "I'll be downstairs in fifteen minutes. I want to talk to you. Meet me in the bar."

I said okay and, after getting checked into the room, I went back downstairs. He was waiting in the bar. He waved me over to a table, and we sat down. I had a ginger ale.

"First of all, Jimmy," he says, once we get settled at the table, "I do want to apologize for some of the things I said earlier. But only some of them. Most of them I believe are true. For instance, the fact that you're a runaway. I could tell that because you don't even have a toilet kit with you on a cross-country hitchhike. You didn't fool me by saying your ride left with your kit. Your clothes look slept in, and I don't know if young people today feel it's more organic to go around smelling like a locker room, but I don't think you've seen a bath in days. Now, I'm going to ask you some questions. I'll know if you're lying. Will you answer me straight if I guarantee you that I won't call any authorities?"

"Deal," I said. Then I told him the whole tale, except for clipping the cash from Aunt Catherine's sugar bowl.

When I finished up, he gives me this funny look and says, "You know, Jimmy, I knew you were in trouble. And as to knowing you were on the run, I recognize the signs. You see, my wife is a great romantic. She'd like to believe that I was a model child in the orphanage. I wasn't. I was more trouble than any kid they ever had at The Moody Home in Elyria. I ran away five or six times. I don't think I ever would have amounted to much. But when the Korean War broke out, I volunteered. And while I was in Korea, being a poor student, I had no specialty in the Army. I was a foot-slogging, dig-a-hole-and-sleep-in-it infantryman. Just another semi-bad kid who was handed a rifle and told where to aim it. But I met some fine people in Korea. Some still living, and the best of them, the one true friend I made, is dead now. He saved my life. Never mind how. Never mind what his name was. It's enough that he was my friend when no one else would be. He wanted to be an architect. He used to tell me how he wanted to design and build. It was his dream. He lost his life for me, and I figured that I owed the man his dream. I decided that if I ever got out of the war alive, I was going to be an architect. The kind that my friend wanted to be."

"And so you done it and made out pretty good, huh?" I asked.

"That would be a swell ending for the story, wouldn't it?" smiled Gaynor. "In a way, it worked out. I went to school intending to be an architect. Took all the courses. But along the way, I discovered I had a flair for industrial design. And, yes, I've done well at it. But I could be an architect if I wanted. I work with architects all the time. Maybe it's wistful, but most of the time, rather than explaining to outsiders what an industrial designer does, I *say* I'm an architect."

Gaynor stopped talking, and I could see his mind was somewhere else. Probably back in Korea. Then he snapped out of it.

"Jimmy," he said, "I'm convinced that you're telling me the truth. It's not for me to pass judgment. Forgive me, that's exactly what I did earlier. What I'm saying is that I'd be happy if you shared our ride to California.

I didn't say nothing for a long time. I thought over what Gaynor had told me. Then I stuck my hand out across the table.

"You got a deal," I said. "But understand. I pay my way. Like, I can't afford no fancy joint like this. After tonight, if you don't mind, I wanna sleep in the car. If you ain't afraid I won't steal nothing."

"I'm not afraid, Jimmy," he said, taking my hand.

And that's how the next day we all was on our way to California together.

4 · The Wreck

I always heard people talk about the wide open spaces. But I never knew what they meant until I saw Texas. Think you could of stood on a chair and seen for fifty miles. I mean, we drove past whole stretches where there wasn't nothing but nothing forever. Once in a while, you'd see these huge piles of rock going way high up in the air. Bill Gaynor said they were buttes and mesas.

But the biggest drag was the music on the car stereo. The Mercedes had this swell AM-FM stereo, but when all you can get is cowboy tunes . . . Well, crap in stereo is still crap. We got tired of hearing all those guys sing through their noses and, after a whole day of it, Bill Gaynor didn't play the radio at all. We switched over to the tape deck, and I was ready for some real neat sounds. No such luck. All the tapes he had were classical. I guess Beethoven is a groove to some people. Myself, I'm more into Fleetwood Mac.

So me and Liz spent a lot of time talking. On account

of the tape playing, we could talk soft and only hear each other. Bill and Ellen Gaynor were into their own rap. Or I ought to say Ellen was. She'd run on, and Gaynor would say "Oh, really?" or "I see" a whole lot.

But I found out a big bunch about the Gaynors from talking with Liz. Like I knew that Bill was doing okay. After all, you don't get a car like he was driving out of a Cocoa Krispies box. Seems Gaynor did so good around Cleveland with his designs that he decided he was going to open an office in Los Angeles. On account of there being so much new construction in California, he was going where the action was and have a vacation along the way.

Liz told me she was let out at first about the family moving. Going to California meant that she wasn't going to graduate with all the kids she went to school with for years. But last year, when Gaynor got the idea to go out west, he took Liz and her mom there for, a vacation. Liz says she took one look at California and decided it was for her.

Then, too, L.A. is where the action is for TV and flicks. Liz wanted to be an actress, like I said. So, even though she was going to miss her friends back in Cleveland, she had figured on going to L.A. once she graduated, anyway.

And, man, how she could rap about acting! I figured I oughta pay close attention, me wanting to be in the same line of work.

"I think that Stanislavsky is the best acting method. That's what Mr. Gruen, my drama teacher, says," Liz tells me.

"Stanis-who?" I said.

"Stanislavsky," Liz says. "He was a top actor in Russia. He wrote a book called *An Actor Prepares*. He tells you how to get inside a character. How to think like that person or role would think."

"What was he, some kind of a mind reader?" I asked. "How's some guy going to tell you how some other person thinks?"

"It's not exactly how another person thinks, Jimmy," Liz says. "It's more how *you'd* think if you were that person. Don't you see?"

I didn't see, but I said "Uh-huh." I was getting to understand how Gaynor worked out talking with his wife. But I did listen close to what Liz was putting down about acting. I found out a lotta stuff I wanted to try out. Once I was alone, anyway. I mean, I'd of felt like a cupcake in front of people doing some of the things Liz said they did in acting class. I can't imagine trying to act like a tree or a leaf. Like that.

But it's the weirdest thing. Even though I knew for the most part Liz was talking a lot of crap, there's something about her that makes you want to listen. I think it's because everything that she does, she does a hundred percent. No hang-ups.

In New York, all the chicks spend a lot of time being cool and hip. They got to let on like they've seen and done it all, and nothing surprises them. And the put-down is a big thing. Even when they're coming on, New York chicks do the put-down thing. Liz isn't like that at all.

She leads with her face. You can tell what's going on in her head by watching her expression just before she says something. Like she telegraphs her punches.

Knowing we couldn't be heard in back, I told her my story. The real one, this time. I told her what it was like living with Uncle Andy; my cousins and all. You should of seen her get mad about the way they dumped on me.

And when I told her about the way I hung one on Uncle Andy, she laughed out loud. It was really something, talking to Liz Gaynor. All the time, I got the feeling that she was hanging on every word, and waiting for the next. After a while, it dawns on me that maybe, just maybe, this girl really cares about me. In a way, it kind of embarrassed me. Nobody else ever cared, and it jerked me around that a girl who only knew me for a few hours would give a crap, one way or another.

And she didn't waste time talking about stuff that doesn't matter. This chick is a deep thinker. I didn't get any gab about who was on the cover of *People* this week. Or who's divorcing who in Hollywood. Like, she went straight at the heart of the bad times I had with my Uncle Andy.

"Jimmy," she says to me, "I think you're a good and sensitive person. You somehow got the idea that you're worthless. Perhaps you listened and, inside, believed you were no good when your family kept saying it, day in and out."

"Don't call them my family," I snapped. "I ain't got a family."

"All right, your relatives, then. But whatever you call them, they've done you damage, emotionally. If you keep telling someone he's no good long enough, after a while he gets to believe it himself."

I didn't say anything for a while. I thought about what she said. The more I thought about it, the better I felt. I mean, I knew what I done was wrong. Hitting and stealing are wrong. And I stole from Aunt Catherine, the one person who never did me wrong. Like, I didn't feel bad about hitting back at Uncle Andy. He was hitting on me when it happened. And I sure didn't care about mushing Jackie's nose all over his face. But Aunt Catherine's money . . . that was different. I told Liz about that.

"You can return the money to her once you get some work, Jimmy," Liz says. "And if your aunt is as good a person as you say, she'll understand why you did it. Do you know? I'll bet she hasn't told your uncle about it at all."

"She couldn't, anyway," I said. Then I explained about her allowance from Uncle Andy.

"Your uncle is a sweetheart, all right," Liz said. "I think if I were your aunt, I would have left with you."

I all of a sudden got a picture of me and Aunt

Catherine out on the road hitchhiking, and I broke up laughing. Liz wanted to know what was so funny, and I told her. We both got a fit of the sillies then. Couldn't stop laughing. Liz did this acting thing where she was Aunt Catherine, and I was hitchhiking with her.

"Jimmy," she says, doing an old lady voice, "No wonder we're not getting rides. Look at your thumb. Dirt under the nail!"

Well, maybe it doesn't sound funny. But the way she said it, I laughed my head off. In fact, I don't remember ever laughing so hard and so often as I did with Liz Gaynor. We were almost rolling around in the back seat, yakking it up. That's when she put her arms around me. Not like she was coming on or anything. It was just like talking wasn't enough any more. It had to be touching. Before I knew it, I had my arms around her, too.

The second I realized what I was doing, I pulled back like a shot. I looked real quick to see if Gaynor and his wife had noticed. But they were still heavy into their own rap. When I looked back at Liz, she was staring at me, almost with tears in her eyes.

"Poor Jimmy," she says, putting her hand on mine. "I didn't mean to embarrass you with that hug. I'm just a physical person, that's all. And I'll bet it's been so long since anyone touched you with real affection that you didn't know how to react."

I let out a laugh that made Ellen Gaynor look over into the back seat for a second. Liz was giving me a hurt face. I said quickly, "Jeez, I'm sorry, Liz. I wasn't laughing at you. I was laughing at me and this situation I'm in. I promise you, I know what to do when a bright, good-looking girl hugs me. I been wanting to do the same thing. But I can't."

"I don't understand," Liz says.

"Listen," I said. "Your old man trusts me. I can't let him down. Here he's giving me a lift to California, not ratting to the cops that I'm on the run, and treating me better than I maybe even deserve. I ain't going to thank him by making a pass at his daughter. But that don't mean I'm made of stone," I added. I checked the front seat once more, and leaned over and kissed her, real fast.

Liz squeezed my hand. "I guess I understand," she said.

We didn't say nothing for the next few miles, then Liz got right back to her ideas about me being starved for love and how lucky she was, having the kind of parents she did.

"I think we're so close as a family," she says, "because Dad never had a real family. And Mommy's mother died years and years ago. Her dad was killed in World War II. Mommy was raised by my grandma. So, in a way, the whole Gaynor family is right here in this car."

"But didn't I hear you mention last night that you got an aunt someplace in California?" I asked.

"That's my Aunt Linda," Liz said. "She's older than

Mommy. She got married when she was seventeen and went to live in California. She and Grandma never got on. She didn't even come to the funeral when Grandma died. Mommy never forgave her."

"Sounds like the kind of family I'm used to," I said.

We were quiet for a while after that. As we was driving along, I started thinking about what she said about me being a good and sensitive person. Nobody ever called me that since my mom died. I felt twelve feet tall. And I made up my mind that when we all got to California, me and Liz was going to stay in touch. Close touch. I don't care what she might of thought about me keeping my distance. But just to let her know I wasn't Frosty the Snowman, we sat real close and now and then snuck a quick hand squeeze.

By dinner, she'd cooled off a little. I guess she hadda. In front of her folks and all. Bill Gaynor was feeling talky for a change. Either that, or Ellen Gaynor finally run out of rap. He was all fulla chatter about the house he had rented in a neighborhood called Brentwood, wherever that is, in L.A. Seems once we got across the desert, which was only a little ways off, he was gonna call the rental outfit and tell 'em to expect them. He seen me looking at him and says, "Silly of me, I suppose. I hate arriving unexpected. I told the rental agency that I wasn't sure how long we'd take to drive cross country. I had thought perhaps we'd stop off here and there. But frankly, I've seen enough of chain restaurants, motels, and automobile graveyards. The countryside isn't the way I remember it.

"Even the little towns have lost all their charm and personality. Time was, you'd know where you were in this country by the look of the buildings and businesses. No more. Even the road signs are the same. And once you're inside another plastic and formica motel, you could be anywhere. I think the time is coming when we'll all look alike, talk alike and, God help us, think alike. I'd like to press on tonight and cross the Arizona desert while the sun is down. There's a full moon, and we should be able to make good time."

"But shouldn't you get some sleep, dear?" asked Ellen Gaynor.

"I'm not at all tired, Ellie," Gaynor says. "And I promise that if I feel drowsy, we'll pull over until daylight. I understand from Jimmy that the car is comfortable enough to sleep in."

He was right. That Mercedes is some car. What I was doing was sleeping in the front passenger seat each night. You grab this handle on the side of the seat, and the seat folds back flat. The seats in that car was more comfortable than the bed I had at my uncle's house. So after dinner, we cleaned up a bit and started out to cross the desert. I still remember the name of that town we left from. Winslow, Arizona it was.

We was halfway across the desert when the Mercedes starts making this noise. I heard it, but I didn't say nothing. I figured it was just something the car did. I mean, I don't know nothing about a big, expensive set of wheels like that. Even when I was in the car alone, I usedta look at all the knobs and crap in front. I couldn't figure out what half the things were for. But Ellen Gaynor knew.

"What's that noise, dear?" she asks Bill Gaynor.

"What noise?" asks Gaynor.

"The car, Bill. It's going t'cunk-t'cunk-t'cunk."

"I don't hear it," says Gaynor.

But right then, we all heard it. The car starts making a real loud, clunking noise. And a red light comes on on the dashboard.

"Uh-oh," says Gaynor. "I think you were right, Ellie. We're losing oil pressure. I don't understand it. I had it checked when we gassed up before leaving." The noise got louder.

"Don't you think we should stop, dear?" asks Ellen Gaynor.

"Out here?" asks Gaynor. "Look around you."

There was a full moon, and you could see the road and the desert real clear. And I mean, there was nothing out there. I couldn't help it, maybe on accounta me being a city person, but I kept thinking about there being lizards and rattlesnakes outside. Yeah, call me a chicken, but snakes and crawly things gimme the creeps. They really do.

Just then, we all spot this sign post. It's a old-fashioned one, too. Like Gaynor said, on the interstate highways, all the signs are the same shape and colors. And they all got this reflector stuff on the letters so's you can read them at night by the light of your headlights. But this was a wood post with a old-fashioned board sign. The paint was old, and the letters was a little hard to make out. Gaynor slowed down, and we woulda missed the turnoff if he didn't.

It was a single-lane road, with no blacktop on it. In the moonlight, you could see it run straight as a string all the way to a little rise in the countryside, maybe two, three miles away down the dirt road. The signpost said CELESTIAL, ARIZ.

Gaynor swung the car onto the dirt road. "There's a town out there, someplace, Ellie," he says to his wife. "I'm going to try to reach it before the engine seizes. I think the oil pump is going."

"But shouldn't we stay on the highway, dear?" asks Ellen Gaynor. "A highway patrol car should be by any time."

"Any time tomorrow morning," answers Gaynor. "I haven't seen so much as a commercial trucker in miles. No, I want to see if we can make it to this Celestial place. I doubt they'll have a Mercedes agency, but they'll surely have a garage and a telephone. "Whoops!"

We went over a dip, and the drop was so sudden, I almost bunked my head on the roof of the car inside. Liz was bounced over, half into my lap. She put her arms around me and stayed there. I wasn't about to complain.

"Bill, if the car is in bad shape, should you drive so fast?" asks Ellen Gaynor.

"We've been driving for six miles," explains Gaynor.

"I think the town has to be just past that rise in the road ahead. If I can get to that rise at a good speed, we can probably coast into the town. Or at least from there, we'll be able to see it."

The car was really making a racket now, and Gaynor gives it a last step on the gas. We musta been doing sixty-five easy when we got over the top of the hill. Once we did, it was too late to do anything.

There was a big barrier. Not those little wood arms with the stripes painted over them. This here thing was about five foot high, with steel pipe anchors on each side and more steel pipes across the narrow one-lane road. And it was set up just at the place where the road cut through the bottom of the hill, with big piles of dirt on both sides.

Gaynor lets out a holler and cuts the wheel to the right, so's he won't hit the barrier. It was too late to put on the brakes. The car hits the pile of dirt on the side of the road, and it was like going up one of those banked turns on a skateboard park. We shot into the air about ten, fifteen feet. I could feel the car start to turn over. I heard Liz scream and felt her hold onto me. I don't know why I did it, but I opened the car door. I maybe had some crazy idea I could get me and Liz out before the car hit the ground.

I dunno if I made it or not. This fat, blue spark jumps in front of my eyes and, brother, I was gonezo!

5 · Karl Horstman Saves My Life

I think it was the pain in my shoulder that woke me up. Or maybe the pain in my head. It felt like a bunch of guys had done a stomp number on me. Then I realized I was laying in a bed! For a crazy couple of minutes, I thought the whole trip, with all that happened, was a coo-coo dream. And that I was back in my bed at my uncle's house in Astoria. I tried to sit up, but I got a terrible pain in my head, and I felt sick to my stomach. A voice said, "Don't try to move, boy. You may be very badly hurt."

I looked around me and things started to come into focus. I was in a narrow bed inside some sort of one-room cabin. But I never saw a joint like this before. For one thing, there was pictures all over the walls. Not in frames, though. And they was all pictures of the desert—the desert in daytime, the desert in moonlight, you name it. And there was a coupla pictures of coyotes and a funny, long-eared rabbit.

In one corner of the room, there was this old-fashioned, black iron stove. It had a big coffee pot on it, and I could smell fresh coffee brewing. There was a huge, round oak table, like you see in Western movies, and sitting at it was this far-out looking dude watching me.

He had a black beard with lots of gray in it and hair that came down to his shoulders. Lotta gray there, too. His eyes was pale gray, and they looked outa his hairy face like two rhinestones in a haystack. He was wearing straight-leg blue jeans and a plaid wool shirt. He had those Indian boots on his feet, you know the kind with silver thingies on the side?

He got up from the table and came towards me. I could see then that he was real tall, maybe six-four, but skinny as a pipe cleaner. He walked over to the bed where I was and grabbed hold of my wrist. I didn't know what was going down, so I tried to pull away.

"Lie still," the weird dude says. "I won't hurt you. I'm a doctor." I laid back in the bed again.

Sure enough, the guy had grabbed my wrist to take my pulse. He rolled back one of my eyelids and stares at my eye, like he was looking for something. Then he holds his left hand in the air with one finger pointed up. "Follow my finger with your eyes," he says. He moved his finger in a straight line from left to right. I did like he said, and I got dizzy. Made my head hurt, too.

"How's your shoulder feel, boy?" the hairy dude asks.

I looked down and for the first time noticed I had this

real neat bandage wrapped across my chest and my left shoulder. There was something hard and stiff, like a piece of wood, under the bandages and across the back of my shoulder. I moved my left arm, and it felt like someone had jabbed me with an ice pick. "Rotten," I said. "It hurts bad when I move."

"Don't move, then," says the guy, smiling. When he smiled, I could see that he had perfect teeth. So white, they almost looked phony.

"This is the point where you're supposed to say, 'Where am I?' 'What happened?' 'Who are you?' " says the hairy dude, still grinning. "To save you the time and effort, I'm Karl Horstman. I'm a doctor, and you're in my cabin, about three miles from Celestial, Arizona. You got here because I carried you. I found you out in the desert two days ago. I don't know who you are or where you came from. Or how you got there. From the marks in the sand where I found you, I could tell that you'd been crawling.

"I saw that your collarbone was fractured. I set and splinted it. I think your ribs on the left side are cracked. That's the tape you feel on your chest. Lucky a lung wasn't punctured. You also have a severe concussion, possible skull fracture, fine-line. I can't tell for sure without x-rays. And the nearest x-ray machine is fifty miles away. That should answer most of your questions."

"There was a car," I said. "Some other people . . ."

"If there was, I didn't see it," said Horstman. "I

found you miles from the nearest road. You're in excellent physical condition and have a remarkable constitution. Most likely it saved your life."

"I gotta get back," I said, remembering the Gaynors. "The people I was with could be bleeding or dying." I tried to sit up again. It just made the pains worse.

Horstman comes over and puts a hand on my chest and pushes me back, but real gentle. "If they were dying, they're dead by now," says Horstman. "I found you two days ago. All you're going to accomplish by moving about is a lot of pain. And you could do yourself some serious harm. A car accident, you say?"

"Yeah. We almost hit a roadblock."

"Roadblock!" says Horstman. "You must mean the Celestial barrier! I found you two miles from there. Two miles of crawling in the shape you were in . . . You have more than a remarkable constitution. It verges on textbook stuff."

"But I gotta find the others!" I said. "They could be dead or dying."

"I wouldn't press it, boy," said Horstman. "If the accident happened at the Celestial barrier, the car's been found. They open the barrier each day for the mail truck to come in. If anyone's alive from the accident, they're in Celestial now."

"Then call 'em up," I says. "Right away. I gotta know!"

Horstman laughed. "I could stand outside the cabin door and holler, boy. But I doubt they'll hear me three miles away. And shouting is as close as you're going to get to a telephone out here."

"What kinda joint is this?" I said. "No phones?"

"Whatever kind of joint it is, boy, it's surely not New York," says Horstman. "You *are* from New York, aren't you?"

"Howdja know?" I asked.

Horstman laughed again. "Because you have a New York accent that you couldn't dent with an ax, is why. Get some rest, boy. If you're all that concerned, I'll be going into Celestial this morning. I was due to go yesterday, but I wanted to wait until you regained consciousness. For a while, I was wondering if you were going to make it. You've been badly hurt, boy."

"Jimmy," I says. "Jimmy Hunter."

"All right, then, Jimmy," Horstman says. "Try to rest. I'll get Rowena saddled and try to find out what happened to the rest of your party."

"Saddled?" I yelp. "You telling me you go around on a horse?"

"You're a long way from the Big Apple, Jimmy," says the hairy guy named Horstman. "And Rowena isn't a horse. She's a burro. Not enough grazing for a horse out here."

"Oh, swell," I says. "A donkey. You won't get there for ages."

"Time doesn't have the same values out here in the desert," he says. "And as to the rush, as I said, if your friends are dead from the accident, it doesn't matter when I get there. They'll wait. If they're still alive, they're being cared for in Celestial."

Horstman went over to a cupboard that was over a sink in the far corner of the cabin. It was a funny sink, too. Didn't have no faucets. Just a pump, like in the flicks. He opens up the cupboard, and I could see a lotta medicine bottles inside. Maybe this weird dude really was a doctor, like he said. He comes out with a throwaway needle, the kind they give you flu shots with. Then he comes over to me. I seen the needle and started backing away. But Horstman just laughs at this.

"Don't worry. I'm not the doctor with the black bottle. This is Demerol. It's a pain killer. You'll be able to sleep without your injuries waking you first time you roll over or move. You need rest more than anything else. This will help you get it."

He had a little foil pack in his hand that I didn't notice before. He tears it open and inside, there's a gauze patch, soaked in some kind of antiseptic. He swabs my arm with it, then lets me have a shot of the Demerol stuff in the needle. Didn't hardly feel it, either. The guy had good hands with a spike.

"There," he says. "You'll start to feel better in a few seconds."

I don't know what he meant by the black bottle crack, but he sure was right about the few seconds part. His face got all blurry, then it felt like my bed started a slow spin that got faster and faster. It was like in the movies, where you see someone caught in a whirlpool.

I went spinning down, down, down. I was out before I hit the teeny, pointy part of the whirlpool at the bottom.

I woke up with Horstman holding my head while I puked into a kidney-shaped basin he was holding under my chin. "It's the Demerol," he says. "Turns some people queasy when they wake up."

"You mean you didn't leave yet?" I yelp in between heaves.

"I've been and come back, Jimmy," Horstman says. "We'll talk once I get you cleaned up. Think you can make it outside to the john?"

"I gotta," I says. "Ain't nobody gonna help me to the can."

"Suit yourself," says Horstman. "I've been bed-panning you for two days now. Once more won't make any difference."

I must have turned red. I mean, I never been so sick in my life that I couldn't make it to the can. Now this guy tells me he's been putting a bedpan under me for two whole days. And cleaning me up, too. I guess that was okay when I was out of it. But now that I was awake, I was gonna handle things myself. I thought.

I sat up on the edge of the bed, and the room spun around. With Horstman helping me, I got up and took two steps. Then I passed out. As I was fading away, I remember seeing Horstman's bright, white smile as he grabbed me under the arms. Then gonezo.

When I woke up, I smelled food cooking. For the

first time in I don't know how long, I was hungry. I didn't know what he was making for a meal, but it smelled great. I sat up and this time, it didn't hurt my head or make me dizzy. My shoulder hurt like a bastard, though.

Horstman was over by the stove, stirring something in a big enamel pot. That's where the good smells was coming from. He must of heard me moving. He turns around and gives me a grin.

"Well, hello again, Jimmy," he says. "Ready for some lunch?"

"I could eat something," I says. "I slept through breakfast, huh?"

"That was yesterday, Jimmy," says Horstman gently. "You've been asleep for twenty-six hours. Let me check you out."

Horstman came over and put me through the same drill he did two days before. Like with following his finger with my eyes. Only this time, it didn't make me dizzy or queasy. He did a couple of more tests, and then he says to me, "No doubt about it, Jimmy. I'm afraid you're going to live."

He helped me up from the bed and over to the table. I was glad it wasn't no big walk. I don't think I would of made it. I plumped down in one of the two chairs he had set up at the table.

Horstman put out two enamel plates and took some biscuits out of the stove. Then, he brings over the big pot and ladles out this great-smelling stew. I got right into it and polished off two plateful. By the time I got done eating, I was feeling pretty normal.

"Great stew," I says. "What kind is it?" Meaning, I figure it came out of a can like Dinty Moore's or Campbell's.

"Stew?" snorts Horstman. "That, my boy, was my best *Civet Lapin.* I'm afraid you're no gourmet."

I thought about the Hounds and Hare Inne with the Gaynors. And not knowing what half the stuff on the menu was, like *filet mignon.*

"It tastes like stew," I said. "But it's *See-vay Lah-pan,* huh? What's that in English, Doc?"

"Please don't call me Doc, Jimmy," says Horstman. "I don't practice medicine anymore. And even when I did, I despised that term. You can call me Karl, or Horstman. But not Doc." He sat there for a second, like his mind was someplace else. Then he says, "As to the *Civet Lapin,* in English it's called rabbit stew. But actually, it bears the same relationship to rabbit stew that a Beef Wellington does to a Big Mac."

I didn't say a word. To tell you the truth, I was trying for all I was worth not to puke my guts up. Jeez! Eating rabbits! But before I knew what it was, it had tasted great to me. I managed not to toss. Horstman must of seen the look on my face, on account of he starts in laughing like mad.

"This isn't a restaurant, Jimmy," he says. "I hunt for most of my fresh meat. But for your information, you would have paid a great deal of money for this meal in a French restaurant."

"Yecch!" I says. "That's the French. They're crazy,

anyhow. They eat frogs and snails, too. No way you get me to eat this crap again!"

"All right with me," says Horstman, getting himself another plateful of rabbit. "But most of the game out here *is* rabbit. Perhaps you would have preferred *Hasenpfeffer,* or Jugged Hare?"

I don't eat nothing with hair on it, I tell him. And that really cracks him up laughing. Once he gets done yakking it up, I ask him, "All right. It's funny. But what happened to the Gaynors?"

I could tell by the look on his face that the news wasn't good. Or I oughta say, from the look in his eyes. With the long hair and beard, you couldn't see that much of his face.

"I hope you can take this, Jimmy," he says. "The two adults that were in the car are dead. The car shot up the embankment near the barrier and landed upside down. Evidently, you and the girl were thrown clear before the car landed."

"You mean Liz is still alive?" I hollered. I was sorry I did. It made my head hurt again. I was half out of my chair.

"Easy, easy. Sit down," says Horstman. "Yes, she's alive. And not badly injured. She was shaken up, and she's still in shock. She doesn't know yet that her parents are dead. The good burghers of Celestial allowed me to examine her, though."

"What does the doctor in town have to say?" I asked.

"The same thing he says right here," says Horstman, pointing a thumb at his own chest. "I'm the only doctor

within fifty-odd miles of here. The people of Celestial
don't believe in doctors. They're a bunch of narrow-
minded, tunnel-visioned, Bible-thumping bigots. Perhaps if I'd been able to get to the two adults in time, I
could have helped. I can't say." Karl Horstman wiped
his face with his hands. "Ah, what's the use?" he says.
"In any event, the girl is alive and, physically, she'll be
fine in a few days."

"I got to go see her," I say, getting up.

"Out of the question, in your condition," says
Horstman.

"But I'm okay now," I say, "I can make it into
town."

"Perhaps you could, Jimmy," Karl says, "You're a
remarkable physical specimen. But the Celestians
wouldn't let you see her."

"What are you talking about?" I say. "Now, how are
they gonna stop me from seeing Liz?"

"The same way they stop anyone but me from
entering Celestial," Karl says. "They'll drive you away.
Oh, they won't shoot at you. They don't believe in
firearms. But they will stone you. They're quite Biblical
that way. They stone transgressors, just like in the
Testaments."

"Like Saint Stephen?" I asked. That's something I
do know about. After all the years with Uncle Andy, I
got a whole headful of Bible readings.

"Exactly, Jimmy," says Horstman, like he was
surprised I'd know.

"What are they, a buncha loonies?" I asked.

"So far as I'm concerned, they're worse than that," says Karl. "A deranged person doesn't realize the harm he does to others or himself. These folks in Celestial should know better. They get mail and merchandise from the outside world, yet they live like a bunch of semi-civilized fools. Right out of the nineteenth century. It's all part of their so-called religion."

"You mean, like those people in Pennsylvania, the ones with beards and all?" I asked.

"The Mennonites?" Karl says. "Not really. They're agrarian socialists, a hangover from the days when such colonies flourished in Oneida and certain areas of Southern Calif . . ." Karl stopped talking when he seen I didn't have idea one of what he was saying. "Let me put it this way, Jimmy," he says, "These people are so bound up in themselves and their religion that they don't want any outsiders to contaminate the purity of their community. They believe in faith healing, too. In Celestial, if you break a leg, they'll know how to set the bone, roughly. But all you'll get to prevent infection in a wound is a Bible reading."

"Then they *are* a bunch of crazies," I said.

"Not insane, Jimmy," Karl says. "If everyone in a society acts the same way, to each other they're not insane. Then, they're just good, God-fearing members of that society, don't you see?"

"No, I don't," I say. "Crazy is crazy, no matter how."

"Ignorant and dangerous, but not insane," says Karl.

"You should be thankful your girl friend had no internal injuries. She would have died with no more attention than a group of those fools standing around the bed singing psalms!" Karl was getting heated up, I could tell.

"Then we gotta get her out of that screwy town," I say.

"I can't see how," says Karl. "The Celestians have her whole life story. When I spoke with Josiah Craig, the head of their church, and he's also the mayor of Celestial, he was quite adamant. You see, they know there's no one expecting her in California, and she won't be missed with both parents dead. Rather than let her go back to the 'world of sin and perdition,' as Craig calls it, they intend to keep her in Celestial. And they further intend to induct her into their lunatic church!"

6 · Karl's Story

"But that's kidnapping!" I yelled. "It's against the law, what they're doing!"

"True, Jimmy," says Horstman. "But to whom does the detained person complain? The sheriff? The mayor? In Celestial, they're one and the same person, Josiah Craig. And Josiah Craig is the head of the True Church of Celestial."

"Well, how about the next town over?" I asked.

"Not a bad idea," Karl says. "The next town is twenty-five miles down the highway, if you head southwest. If you head back east, it's eighty-five miles to Winslow. If I were to go, I'd take Rowena and, at that, it'd be a full day's ride in the desert sun. Granted I'd go, which I won't."

"What are you saying?" I yelped. "You mean you'd let those loonies keep Liz there, in their nutty town?"

"Exactly," says Karl Horstman.

"I don't understand where you're coming from, man," I says.

"It's simple, Jimmy," Karl says. "I will not be involved."

"How not involved?" I asked. "You already patched me up. And you went into town to see about Liz."

"I would have been due at the post office in Celestial anyway," Karl says. "From time to time, I go there. I get supplies, things that I can't make or hunt for. And I get my mail, such as it is, from the post office. But make no mistake. I am not going to jeopardize my relationship with Celestians for a pair of kids I don't even know. And as to patching you up, as you put it, that's another matter. I may have resigned from the human race to an extent, but I am still a doctor. You were badly injured; I helped you. But once you're well enough to get around, you're free to do whatever you wish. Provided you don't involve me."

"I don't get it," I says. "You say one thing, then you do another. You tell me how rotten the townies in Celestial are, but it's like you don't care what they do."

"I don't," says Karl.

"Then why'd you even bother to ask about Liz?"

"I didn't have to ask," Karl says. "As soon as I got to Celestial, Craig asked me to look at her. He volunteered the information."

"I don't understand you at all, man," I says.

"You don't have to," snaps Horstman, getting hot. "You are only a minor interruption in my life. The fact that I helped you doesn't imply any sense of obligation to you. Nor you to me. Once you're able to leave, you'll do what you will. Then I'll be alone which, frankly, is how I prefer to be. If that sounds cold, sobeit."

I looked at Horstman and, if he felt bad about what he said, you couldn't tell it from the look on his face. He looked straight at me, with those pale gray eyes, and never flinched or blinked. Like he was daring me to argue with him. But I wasn't gonna be put off.

"What do you think you are, some kinda tin god?" I holler. "Liz Gaynor is the nicest, cleanest chick I ever met in my life. And her folks was great people. I mean, I only knew them for a few days, but they was great people. The best. We got to do something to help Liz!"

"Not *we,* Jimmy, you," says Horstman. "You may feel you have to do something; I do not. I won't interfere with your plans. I'll even tell you all I know about Celestial. But I will *not* be involved!"

Now, there wasn't no way I could explain to Horstman how I felt about Liz Gaynor. But I knew that to get her loose of those coo-coos in Celestial, I had to have Karl Horstman's help. So I went right back at him. I said, "All right, Karl, if you're so uninvolved, why do you even bother to keep all the doctor stuff around? It's part of your number to help people if you're a doctor."

"I was a doctor, once," says Horstman. "But I stopped being a doctor in 1968. All the 'doctor stuff,' as you so quaintly call it, is for me. I'm alone out here and, should I be injured or fall ill, I can treat myself. I neither seek the company of men, nor do I find it particularly pleasant when their company is thrust upon me."

"Meaning me?"

"Meaning you," he says. He got up and started clearing away the dishes from the meal. I got up to help.

"No, no," he says. "You sit. Rest is what you need more than anything else. And the sooner you're healed, the sooner you'll be out of my life."

"Y'know?" I says. "For a guy who picks up hurt strangers and doctors them, you got a strange attitude."

Horstman laughed, but there wasn't any happiness in the laugh. "You may be right, Jimmy," he says. "If you stay put while I clean up this mess, I may just explain it to you. I can see you won't give me any peace until I do. Once you hear, you'll understand and stop bugging me."

Horstman went outside and cleaned the tin plates by jamming them into the sand. He seen me watching and tells me that water is precious out in the desert. That his well goes dry sometimes in summertime. So he cleans his dishes without water. After he finishes cleaning up, he goes to the cupboard where the doctor supplies are. He takes out a big jug of clear fluid and, from under the sink, he gets out an airtight can of pipe tobacco.

"Do you smoke?" he asks from the sink.

"Nah, can't cut the taste," I says.

"Good," he says, sitting down and putting the bottle in front of him on the table. "That makes all the more for me. Do you drink?"

"What is that stuff?" I asked, pointing at the bottle of clear liquid.

"Straight grain alcohol," says Karl. "One hundred-and-eighty proof. Instant drunk and virtually no hangover. It's the impurities that cause hangovers, you know. That and guilt. Which now that I think of it are the impurities of the conscience." And he laughed that unhappy laugh again. He didn't bother with a glass. He took the glass stopper out of the bottle and slugged down two or three gulps. "With ice and an olive, it's a great Martini," he says. "But there's no ice for twenty-five miles, and I've already eaten, so I don't need the olive, either. *Prosit!*"

He took another few glugs of the stuff and lets out a belch. "Now, my boy," he says, "you want to know why I don't get involved anymore. Well, I used to be involved. In the late 1960's. But like the writer, Phil Ochs, said, 'I ain't marchin' any more.' "

I guess what Horstman said about the grain alcohol was right. He had knocked down about four shots of the booze, and already his eyes was all bloodshot. He stuffed his pipe, lit it, and took another slug of the alcohol.

"Oh, did I ever march," he says, grinning like a crocodile. "You name a cause, there was Horstman . . . Excuse me, *Doctor* Horstman, fellow of the

American College of Surgeons, affiliated with Massachusetts General Hospital, brilliant neurosurgeon; a practice in Brookline, a beautiful wife, a handsome son. I had a loaf of bread under each arm so, naturally, I wanted to share my good fortune with the less fortunate."

"What went wrong?" I asked. "Sounds like you were all set."

"Everything went wrong," Horstman says. "Inside of eighteen month's time, my wife developed a brain tumor. Oh, I should have recognized the symptoms. The vagueness, the irritability, the way she'd accidentally transpose words . . . smelling something burning when nothing was. But I was so involved with my free clinic in Roxbury, my civil rights rallies, my organizations, that I didn't see it coming on. By the time I noticed, it was almost too late. Rushed her into exploratory surgery after one look at the x-rays of her skull . . ." Horstman took another shot of the grain alcohol. He was getting pretty boxed now, and his speech was slurred.

"Did you operate on her yourself?" I asked. "I mean, you said you're a surgeon."

"I was a neurosurgeon," Karl admitted. "But not a brain surgeon. Sure, I was trained in that area, but my specialty was more in spinal nerve involvement than cranial. I assisted at the operation. When we saw what was inside, a malignant glioblastoma crowding the cerebral cortex, I . . ." Horstman looked at me and seen I didn't understand. Then he said, "This tumor was smack in the part of the brain that makes you the person you are, Jimmy. And it was too large and heavily rooted to get it all. I suppose it was a blessing that she died on the table. Even if she had survived, she would have been a vegetable for the rest of her life. I blamed myself for it. I should have recognized the symptoms months earlier. But I was too busy out doing good for my fellow man."

"How can you blame yourself for cancer?" I says. I knew what malignant meant from when Mom was sick. "You done your best, didn't you?"

"Ah, but did I?" says Horstman. "Maybe yes, maybe no. It was the doubt that flogged me. I started boozing. And one fine, frosty night on the Massachusetts Turnpike, with five martinis under my belt and my son beside me, I ran into an abutment at sixty miles an hour . . ." Horstman was crying now. I didn't want to let on I saw it. So I didn't say nothing. "I walked away without a scratch. But my son will never walk again. He's with his grandmother in Marlboro. I can't bear to see him. It was my fault. My fault again! My own, stupid, drunken fault!" He put his head down on the table and hid his face, like a little kid does when he cries. He kept talking, but it was hard to get his words between the booze and the tears.

"I bummed around the country after that. And I hated what I saw. Within weeks of my wife's death, Bobby Kennedy and Martin Luther King were murdered. The war in Vietnam went on, students rioting, then the Manson murders. I couldn't take it any more. I admit it; I quit. I bought this place, and I spend my time at painting. I have my music, and . . ." With this, he sat up again and grabbed the bottle of alcohol. "Every other day, about this time, I get quietly and outrageously drunk, until my brain shuts down. My one regret is that I don't have the courage to kill myself outright." He took another shot from the bottle, then he stood up, took two steps toward the door, and passed out.

It hurt my shoulder, but I managed to get him off the floor and over to the one bed in the cabin. He was out and, when I touched him, he felt chilly. I covered him up and, in a while, he begins to snore. I scrounged around in the cabin and found some more blankets and an air mattress. I blew it up, but it took a while, on account of it hurt my ribs to take deep breaths. I spread out the mattress on the floor, next to the bed, and then turned out the Coleman lantern that lit the cabin.

I laid there for a long time in the dark. I kept thinking of Liz. I didn't know how I was gonna swing it, but I knew I had to get her outa there. I fell out then and, the next thing I knew, it was daylight, and Karl Horstman was waking me up.

"Breakfast," he says and walks away to the stove once he sees my eyes are open.

Man, the way he was bopping around the cabin, you'd of never thought he was so totally plotzed the night before. Maybe he was right about grain alcohol not giving you a hangover. He had a pot of coffee going, and there was bacon frying. He took a pan of biscuits out of the oven and, in a few minutes, I did as much damage to the meal as I could. I knew I must of been getting over the hurts. Felt like I was getting stronger with every bite of breakfast I ate.

Karl wasn't feeling talky, so I just ate and didn't say much. After breakfast, he checked out my bandage and made me go through the drill with watching the finger again. He seemed satisfied with what he found.

"Marvelous," he says. "The human body never fails to fascinate me. You're bounding back at a rate that beggars description. Of course, you were obviously in superb condition to begin with. And as you neither smoke nor drink, it's going quickly."

"How long do you figure before I can get around?" I asked.

"Ummm. At this rate, I'd guess about two, three weeks."

"Weeks?" I hollered. "How can you talk about weeks with Liz down there in Celestial?"

"I can talk years if I want to," says Karl, coldly. "You're the one on the time schedule, not me."

"Back to that again?" I ask.

"Back to that," he says. He got up and started clearing the table. "Don't think because I got stewed and maudlin last night that it changes anything. It's like I told you. Anything I care about either dies or gets crippled. I've resigned from getting involved. And nothing you say or do will change that!''

"Okay, okay," I says. "But you said yesterday, you'd tell me what you know about Celestial. I guess I oughta know and have a plan, if I'm gonna get Liz out of there. If she ain't already tried to get out herself. Like, she could be trying to get away right now. I should be helping.''

"She's not going anywhere," Karl says. "Where can she go? It's the same as they don't need walls on Devil's Island. It's six miles to the interstate highway. There's desert all around. She wouldn't get six feet, let alone six miles. I'm sure she's being watched all the time. Celestial is a small town, and everyone knows everyone else's business. They're a cohesive community, Jimmy."

"A what?"

"They stick together," he says. "The only way she'll leave Celestial is with Josiah Craig's permission. And as I told you, that's not about to happen."

Then Karl fills me in on the town of Celestial.

"The town hasn't had any real contact with the outside world in close to a hundred years, Jimmy. They have their own ways and customs of worship. All they ask is to be left alone, which I can well understand," he says, giving me a look like I'm putting him out.

"But what about the wars?" I ask. "World War I and II. The Korean and Vietnam Wars? Didn't anybody from there get drafted or nothing?"

"Religious exemptions from all four," Horstman explains. "Then, too, they're autonomous in Celestial. Had their own draft boards. Not that it would have mattered, anyway. Most of them are congenitally unfit for service in the armed forces."

I didn't know what con-whatchimicallit unfit was, and I said so to Horstman. He explains. "Birth defects, Jimmy. It's hard to find a whole, unmarked person in all of Celestial. Twisted spines, color blindness, hunchbacks, clubfeet, hemophilia. You name it, you can find it in Celestial."

"But how come? Why?" I ask.

"The town has a population of about two hundred, Jimmy. And there are only six families: the Craigs, the Stones, the Williams . . . I forget the others. In any event, they have been intermarrying for close to a hundred years. Every soul in Celestial is really a cousin of one degree or another. And when the genetic pool of a group is so finely interconnected, any flukish strain in their germ plasm comes to the surface."

"You mean," I ask, "like if cousins marry, the kids are crazy? I heard that from my Uncle Andy. He says it's in the Bible that you can't marry your second cousin."

"It is good genetic practice," says Horstman. "Then again, it's not necessarily true, either. In a good number of societies, past *and* present, cousins, even brothers and sisters, marry. And often have healthy children. But because of tribal practices in many of these societies of stealing wives from other tribes, the genetic pool doesn't stagnate, as it does in Celestial. It's become so bad in that town that hardly any children are born alive. Even when the women can conceive. And those that are born alive are all deformed in one way or another. Maybe even Josiah Craig recognizes that. Josiah may feel that Liz represents new breeding stock."

I came out of my chair for that one. "No way!" I hollered.

"Sit down, sit down," says Karl, annoyed. "You aren't strong enough to walk to Celestial, let alone do anything. If you insist you're fit, I'll show you how strong you are. I have some hunting to do this morning. If you can keep quiet and stay out of my way, I'll take you."

He went over to the wall and took a wool shirt off a hook. He tossed it to me. All this time, I been sitting around in my jeans and bare feet. When I was laid out, Karl must of undressed me.

"Wear this," he says. "I had to cut your T-shirt off you after I found you. This shirt will fit over that splint on your shoulder. Just tuck up the sleeve. Your sneakers are under the bed, along with your socks."

Lucky that Horstman is a big dude, even if he is skinny. The shirt almost fit me. Horstman went outside the shack while I got my shoes and socks on. When I came out, he had a steel rod with a handle on it, like a golf club. But the end wasn't like a golf club. It had a rounded hook. He had a big burlap sack in his hand.

But I didn't see no rifle, and he was supposed to go out hunting. I thought about last night's rabbit stew and asked, "What are we hunting for, Karl? More rabbits?"

"No," he says. "Rattlesnakes!"

7 · Where Do You Sit When You Milk a Snake?

Karl saddled up the donkey for me to ride. He told me how to sit and that the donkey was gentle. I wasn't gonna ride while he walked, and I told him so.

"You couldn't keep up with me," he says. "I'm used to walking, anyway. I wouldn't have taken Rowena if I were going alone. The terrain is rough. Don't worry, we'll come to a place where we'll have to leave her. You'll get in more than enough walking. Then, at least, you'll know what I mean about your not being fit to go to town.

I went along with what he said. I mean, there wasn't no point in arguing. We made toward a line of hills that seemed to get further away the more we traveled. As we went along, Karl kept filling me in on Celestial. But I was only listening with half an ear. I kept thinking about what he said. Hunting rattlesnakes!

"So, you see, when Josiah Craig's grandfather

founded the True Church of Celestial, they shut the town off to any outsiders. By the instruction of God, if you can believe what Craig says."

"Say, listen, Karl," I says. "I know I should learn about this town full of loons and all but, honest, are we really going after rattlesnakes? And what for?"

"Why, they're good eating, Jimmy," Horstman says with a grin.

"Not for me, they ain't!" I yelp. "I can't even look at snakes. You're gonna have to break my other shoulder to get me to eat a snake. And besides, ain't they poison?"

"The poison glands are in the head, Jim," he says. "And you don't eat the head. There's no poison in the body. The meat is quite tender. Sort of a cross between frog's legs and chicken."

"Forget it!" I says. "I'll take your word for what it's like. But I ain't eating any rattlesnake! What do you want to eat it for, anyway?"

"Actually, I go after rattlers for two reasons," Karl says. "I do eat the meat but, primarily, it's for the venom that I hunt them. I make an anti-venom serum from it. That is, with Rowena's help."

"Huh?"

Then Karl explains to me that with a series of small shots of rattlesnake venom that won't hurt the donkey, he makes a serum that helps to cure snakebites. He trades off stuff like this and doctoring the farm animals in Celestial for bacon, butter, and other stuff he can't grow out where he is.

"Funny thing," I says. "The townies'll let you treat their animals, but not them. Don't that strike them odd, either?"

"I suppose it should," Karl admits. "But Craig is a bit more flexible than some of the other members of the church down there. In fact, when he broke his leg in the mine, I set it for him. He gave me Rowena in return for that."

"Excuse me, Karl, but what mine is that?" I ask.

"It's an abandoned lead mine," he says, pointing off aways, "right where these hills we're in come down to form the Celestial valley. It's somehow sacred to the townies. According to Craig, God appeared to his great-grandfather there, about a hundred years ago."

"You gotta be kidding," I says. "*God* appeared in a lead mine?"

"I didn't say I believed it, Jimmy. I'm only repeating what Josiah Craig told me. That was back when he thought I might join their church. You see, when I began getting mail at their post office addressed to Dr. K. Horstman, Craig threw out the idea that I might join the community. I nearly had some trouble right then and there. Told him I was an atheist, and all I wanted was to be left alone. That was eight years ago. Since then, we coexist, but Craig is the only one who has contact with me. Except, of course, when someone is injured, and I treat him or her."

"It still sounds screwy to me," I says. Karl was quiet for a few minutes. Then he says to me, "Okay, Jimmy. From here we walk."

I got down off the donkey, and Karl tied the reins to a bush. Funny, I figured the desert would be all sand, with nothing growing, like in them Foreign Legion movies. I asked Karl about it. He told me that part of the desert *is* like that, but nobody lives there. The parts where folks live, they got some underground water, and plants do grow. But there ain't enough water or rain to raise food or even a scruffy tree. I even found out it rains in the desert. Karl said it's something to see. On account of just before it rains, the desert looks all dead. But inside of twenty-four hours after it rains, all of a sudden, the whole place is blooming with flowers and stuff. He says that the little rain they get is all the plants need to bloom, seed, and keep going until the next rain. But Celestial is in a little valley, and they got underground water from wells. They irrigate and they grow what they need.

Karl is telling me all this while we're walking. After a few minutes, I start to see what he meant about me keeping up with him. Like, I almost make two of this guy. True, he's about four inches taller than me, but I easy outweigh him by twenty pounds. I swear that dude is made of steel springs and leather, not skin and bone. He don't ever get tired! By the time we got where we was going, Karl is still chirping like a bird and man, my butt was really dragging!

No way I was gonna ask him to slow down, but I don't mind saying that when he all of a sudden stops and motions me to be quiet, I was one happy person. I sat down on a rock. Karl grabs my good arm and brings me over to another rock, where he's looking over the edge, down below, to a big, flat space in the hills.

"Look down there," he says, pointing at a rock where the sun is shining down. "Can you see them?"

I looked where he was pointing but didn't see anything. Then I saw them. One moved. My skin crawled. There was maybe five or six rattlesnakes down there! I didn't notice them at first on account of their colors. Funny, when you see a rattlesnake in the zoo, you tell yourself you'd never miss seeing one. They have these bright diamond markings on their backs. But when they're out where they live, in the desert, you could almost step on one without seeing it. That's how good they blend in.

"How you gonna get them?" I whispered to Karl.

"You don't have to whisper, Jimmy," Karl says. "Rattlers can't hear. They'll pick up vibrations through the ground or smell you, but they can't hear. No ears. Now sit still and watch."

I looked as Karl went down the hillside and circled around to where the snakes was laying in the sun. I gotta admit he was slick. Before any of the snakes was on to the fact he was there, he had one real monster scooped up on the end of his golf club hook, and squirming. He popped the creepy thing right into his burlap bag, and that was it. In a few minutes, he came back to where I was, but stood off aways.

"Got a good one. Must be five feet long," he says.

"You follow me. I have to give a wide berth to Rowena when we get back to where she's tethered. If she gets wind of the rattler, she may panic."

I didn't tell him that I wasn't too happy about being close to a five-foot rattlesnake, either. So I just followed him, like he said to.

When we got back to the cabin, Karl did one of the scariest things I ever saw. With the big hook and a pair of heavy gloves, he gets the rattler out of the sack and on the ground. Then before the rattler could coil up, he's somehow got the creepy thing by the back of the head, so's it can't bite him.

He goes over to the table where he's got this jar, like you see in lab at chemistry class, and he fits the snake's teeth, the two big fangs, over the lip of the jar. In no time, I can see the poison running down the side of the jar and into its bottom. He got a lot of juice out of that snake, too. Karl said it was enough to maybe kill a horse! That's when he did this thing that I still can't believe.

When he's all done milking the snake, he twirls the thing over his head, like a big rope. Then he cracks it! Just like a whip. When he did, the big rattlesnake's head pops right off! While the thing is still crawling, but without a head, he starts in skinning the monster. I couldn't watch much after that.

To make things weirder, all the time he's doing this, he's telling me about the town of Celestial and the people who live there. Like he wasn't milking a snake; maybe eating breakfast or brushing his teeth. I found it hard to pay attention to all he was saying, because I couldn't take my eyes off that rattler.

He even cooked the snake up for a side dish at dinner that night. I don't have to tell you that I didn't eat any. But I learned at lot about Celestial and Karl, too.

Karl plays the flute. Pretty good, too. But he don't play stuff like Ian Anderson in Jethro Tull. He plays classical. For the most of it, I didn't dig the music. I mean, it was good, and he played fine. Just that there wasn't much tune to what he did. Except one piece I liked. Karl told me it was by Mozart. He was tickled that I liked it. Seems it was his favorite, too.

And what I learned about Celestial was an eye opener. If Karl hadn't drawn a map of the town, I would of been in big trouble. See, I was ready to go storming down there, scout around, find Liz, and somehow get back to the main highway. I figured that from there, we could flag down a passing car or truck.

Karl shook his head when I told him what I had in mind. "You'd never get to the highway, Jimmy," he says. "You'd have to get her out of where she's being kept with no one getting wise. That means at night, while the town is asleep. And the road back to the main road is the first route they'd check. All Josiah Craig has to do is saddle his horse and follow the road to find you."

"Then do you have a better idea?" I ask.

"Go cross country," he says. "Make for Martinsville. By the main highway route, it's twenty-five miles. But if you go cross country, it's more like fifteen."

"Fine. I go across the desert at night," I say. "But how can I tell I'm going right? Ain't any signs or lights at all."

"I have a pocket compass I can let you have," Karl says. "If you study this map I've drawn, you can see how to travel. But you must travel at night. In the daytime, the sun would fry you both to a crisp in no time at all."

I could see that Karl had it thought out better than I did. So, for the next coupla weeks, all I did was study the map he made. It helped pass the time. Mostly, what I wanted to do was let Liz know I was still alive, and not to give up hope.

The day Karl took the bandage and splint off my shoulder, I told him I was ready to go. "Don't be hasty," he says. "All you've seen so far is the town of Celestial on a map."

"I got it down cold," I tell him. "I can close my eyes and still see that map."

"It'll be a lot different when you see it," Karl says. "I'm due in Celestial today, and you can come with me as far as the edge of the valley. I have a pair of binoculars. You can scout the terrain from above in the daylight. That way, there'll be no surprises in the dark."

I looked at Karl across the table in the cabin where we had the map spread out. "I want to thank you, Karl," I says. "You been doing a lot for me. I won't forget."

What showed of Horstman's face through all the hair got red. "Self-preservation, kid," he says. "If you get caught, and the townies find out you're from the same car wreck as your girl friend, they'll know where you've been. With me. And there goes my relationship with Craig, the whole town. So, don't thank me. Just don't get caught, that's all!"

I could see I was putting him uptight by being grateful, so I didn't press it. In a while, he had all his act together. He took the anti-venom he made from the rattler he killed. "My excuse to visit town," he explains.

It took about an hour to get to the place where the hills overlooked Celestial. Karl said we could of gone an easier way, but the townies might of spotted me. I put the glasses to my eyes and watched from up above while Karl went into the town.

There was maybe thirty houses in Celestial. All of the town is built around this one building. I know from the map that it's their town hall and church combined. And all the houses are built exactly the same. They're two stories high, like square boxes with pointy roofs. The roofs got unpainted shingles, and the sides are painted white. There's shutters on the windows, and all the shutters are painted blue. Even the same shade of blue. Like each house was made from a cookie cutter. But when I got to see the people in Celestial, I really got the creeps.

From where I was and with the binoculars, I could

see them as good as if they was across the street. And
when I did, I was sorry I could. There was something
awfully wrong with every living person I saw. And I saw
maybe ten, fifteen people in the street that day.

The first one I saw, it took me a few seconds to tell if
it was a man or a woman. Or even human. But it was
wearing a dress, so I guess it was female. She only had
one eye and, where she should of had a nose, there was
two holes in her face, with bright pink skin all around
the holes. The rest of her face was dead white, except
for the right cheek. It was covered with a huge, hairy
birthmark that was deep purple. Her spine was twisted
up, so she had to walk with a cane, and she moved kind
of with a sideways motion. Like a crab. It must of been
hard for her to get around on account of just walking
made her breathe hard. She walked with her mouth
open, to breathe better, I guess, and I could see a shiny
line of drool that ran down the corner of her mouth. It
dripped onto her black dress, and I could see a darker
spot where it soaked in.

I thought at first that she might of been the town
freak or something. But then I saw the others. If you
can believe it, the one I saw first wasn't the worst one! I
could tell you about the other horror shows, no sweat,
but I don't know if you'd believe me. Sometimes I
can still see them in my dreams. I nearly puked when
I saw them. Karl was right. I had to scout the town
first. If I would of run into one of those half-human
things in the dark, I woulda jumped clean out of my

skin! All the townies looked like aliens right out of a sci-fi flick.

Then, I see this real big dude come out of the church-town hall building. Just as Karl Horstman got to the center of town on his donkey. He comes down the stairs to the street, where Horstman is. This dude was almost human looking. Like the other townies, he's dressed in a black suit, white shirt, and a black tie. He's wearing a kind of cowboy hat, but with the top of it low and round. The hat brim was straight out, all around, like a plate. He's got a beard, but it don't cover up the whole side of his face that's got a big blotch of purple on it. He's got a big, fleshy *thing,* a growth, I guess, that hangs down the blotch side of his face, like the red things on a turkey's neck. Almost like he was growing a hairy, purple apple out of his cheek.

He walked with a limp, and his right shoulder was all twisted up to make him a hunchback. Then my heart nearly stopped. Coming behind him out of the church is this woman. She's dressed like all the other townies. Black dress, with a long skirt and an old-fashioned black bonnet. But she ain't any monster like the rest. She's walking right and, when she turns her head, I could see it was Liz!

She seemed like she was in a daze, the way she walked behind this horror show dude. The big guy stops, and he begins talking with Horstman. Liz hangs back, like she was afraid to go near Karl. I knew right then that this scary-looking guy has to be the leader of the town, Josiah Craig. Karl already told me that Josiah Craig is big, and that he's the only one in the town Karl's allowed to deal with.

They rapped for a while in the street and walked about a half block. They turned in and went into a house. I knew from Karl's map that it was the Craig house. They stayed in there for an hour it seemed. I couldn't stand to see any more of those monsters, so I just laid up in the sun and waited for Karl to come back. When he did, we walked in silence for the rest of the hike back to his cabin. Once we was there, Karl goes and gets out his jug of grain alcohol and takes a stiff knock. He holds out the jug to me, and I had a knock, too.

Man, talk about drinking lighter fluid! That stuff almost took my head off. I managed not to choke or toss, but I felt like doing both. After the flames stopped shooting out of my ears, a big warm spot built up in my chest and stomach. It was only then that Karl said, "Pretty grim, isn't it?"

"Grim?" I yelp. "I almost puked! You telling me that they look that way because cousins been marrying cousins for a hundred years? Man, they sure are doing *something* wrong!"

"It doesn't show at first, Jimmy," Karl says. "But I suppose it's been building gradually, over the years."

"But how can they even look at each other?" I ask.

"I guess that when everyone in town is deformed, you don't notice," Karl says. "Like the old saying that goes, 'I didn't know we were poor when I was a kid, because everyone else in the neighborhood was poor, too.' When what's normal is hideous, hideous becomes commonplace and no longer offputting. At least that's my theory."

"But, Liz," I say. "She must be going through some trip! I seen her when you and Craig was talking. Looked like they got her brainwashed or something. Or like she was hypnotized."

"She's in bad emotional shape, Jimmy," Karl says. "And it's understandable. When you consider that she's lost both her parents. By the way, Craig has told her they're dead. Then she wakes up to find herself in a horror film that's real and inescapable. Why, I think I'd be in rough shape, too."

"I'm going to get her out tonight!" I say, making up my mind right then. "I can't let her spend another day there!"

"Whoa, whoa!" says Karl. "I don't know if you're in shape yet. And on top of that, it isn't a good night for it. There's a full moon. In the desert, that's quite bright. You'd be spotted."

"I don't care!" I holler. "She could go nuts down there. And she don't even know that I'm alive. Or did you tell her?"

"I couldn't, Jimmy," Karl says. "I wasn't alone with her at all. You were right, by the way. She's tried to escape twice. She never got far. But now, they have a watch on her. She's staying in the Craig house. In a downstairs bedroom, behind the kitchen. It has a lockable door. Here, let me draw you a plan of the house.''

Karl draws up a blueprint, like, of the Craig house. I can see then what he means. They got no locks on the doors in Celestial, he explains. On account of they got no crime. Everyone belongs to the church, and everyone owns everything together. Like, if you wanted something somebody else had, you only got to ask. But all the pantries and storerooms got outside latches on the doors. The Craigs are keeping Liz in a pantry-bedroom setup, on account of her trying to get away.

"What about the window to the pantry?" I ask.

"It's got a mesh screen across it from the outside," Karl says. "To keep the wildlife from breaking in. Coyotes, ground squirrels, and such.'' He pointed to the plan he was showing me. "Your big edge is that no one knows you're coming to get her. A certain amount of noise would be written off as an animal trying to get into the pantry. It's not uncommon.''

"What about watchdogs?" I asked. "I didn't see any dogs in town.''

"That's because there aren't any," Karl says. "Don't ask me why. But there are no pets of any description in Celestial. Maybe their lunatic religion forbids them as a frivolity. I wouldn't know. And I wasn't ever curious enough to ask.''

"Then I'm going down there tonight," I says.

"Foolish," Karl says.

"Maybe so," I says, "but I gotta do it."

"I can't talk you out of it?" Karl says.

"No way!"

"Then if there is a god," Karl says, "may He help you!"

8 · Celestial by Moonlight

Karl helped me put together my stuff. My leather jacket was still okay, but my old T-shirt was ripped up from when Karl set my shoulder. My jeans were okay. I'd been wearing them. And my sneakers were in good shape. Karl told me I could have the wool shirt I'd been wearing.

He gave me back what was left of my money and my wallet. He had put them away for me while I was out of it after the accident. He was gonna give me more, but I told him I was okay. I figured I had enough for when we got to Martinsville. And if we got caught by the townies, well, I wouldn't need no money then. When I had all my stuff together, Karl goes over to the sink cupboard and puts some pills in a bottle for me.

"The white pills are multiple vitamins, Jimmy," he tells me. "And those small, orange pills are amphetamines. If you think hiking fifteen miles across the desert is easy, you're wrong. You may be badly fatigued. The amphetamines will keep you going. Take four of these vitamins now. And I guess I can spare you one of my canteens. But if you're in any danger of being caught, you toss that thing as far away as possible, understand? The townies would recognize it as mine. Then I'd be in trouble myself."

I promised to do just like Karl said. He filled the canteen from the pump at the sink, and I was ready to go. I stood at the door. It was real dark now but, like Karl said, with the moon coming up, parts of the outside was bright as a cloudy day. I knew I had to get going. Karl was at the table with his jug of alcohol, not even looking my way.

"Well, so long, Karl," I says. "And thanks for all you done, the doctoring, the maps . . . all of it."

"I told you why I did it," he says, still not looking up. "You don't have to thank me, just leave me in peace. And don't get caught with my canteen!" Then he has another knock of juice and stares at the wall. No handshake, no "see yuh around." Nothing.

Feeling kind of let out, I closed the cabin door behind me. I was walking away toward Celestial, when I turned around and looked back at the cabin. I was kind of hoping I'd see Karl in the window. Like he could of waved or something. But no.

I started walking again. Then I heard Karl playing the flute. Sound carries in the desert. He was playing the Mozart tune I liked. Maybe it was as close as a guy like Karl can get to saying good-bye.

Boy, was Karl right about the desert being tricky at

night. The full moon wasn't all the way up in the sky, and it threw funny shadows. I'd already seen the trail to Celestial and walked it, but I still missed my footing and fell a couple of times before I made it down the hill into town.

The trail ended on the other side of the burg. I had to circle the outskirts before I could come up near the town hall-church building where Craig's house was. All the lights in Celestial was out except for one—Craig's place.

When I got to the house, I scaled the low picket fence and squinched close to the outside wall. I figured that if I was real close to the side of the house, even if someone stuck his head out a window, they'd have to look straight down to see me. And when somebody looks out a window, they don't usually glance that way.

It was a good thing I stayed close to the wall. I was right under the window where the light was on. I nearly dropped one when the window above me opens! I looked up and there, close enough to touch, was Josiah Craig. I could see the big, ugly, hairy growth on his face. The light from behind him and the full moon made him look even creepier, if that's possible. I don't know why he opened the window just then, but I plastered myself to the side of the house like a coat of paint. In a second, he pulled his head back in, and I could hear voices from inside. I took a chance and sneaked a look in through the opened window.

There were three people in the room. It was the

parlor, and it was furnished real plain. Like what you see in museums of what old-timey folks lived in. There was a big Bible on a stand; a couch that had no cushions, made of some plain wood. There was some straight-back chairs and a round, hooked rug on the bare, wooden floor. The walls had a lot of these needlepoint things in frames. They wasn't pictures; they had sayings on them like GOD BLESS THIS HOUSE and all. It was kind of nice in a plain way. The only thing that spoiled it was two of the people in the room.

Josiah Craig up close was even bigger than he looked through the binoculars. I'd say he was about Karl's height, but easy fifty pounds heavier. You could see that the purple blotch with the apple-sized growth on it really started well below his collar and went all the way up past his hairline. His big, thick beard didn't hide much. He was dressed like when I first seen him, but he had his suit coat off.

Across from him was a lady who wasn't as screwed up physically as the one-eyed, no-nosed woman I seen. But she came close. From the way she was sitting, I could see she was a hunchback, too. She had two eyes, but they was set wrong in her face. One a lot higher than the other. She had a purple birthmark, too. But it didn't have no growth coming out of it like Josiah Craig's.

I guess the woman's looks gave me the creeps because she was close to looking human, but still wasn't. It was only that everything about her, physical- ly, was just a shade *wrong*. Like, she had her black bonnet off and her hair was pulled back in a bun. Fine, except that she had big patches of white in her black hair, and two or three bald spots that no amount of combing was going to disguise. And sitting in between the creepy woman and Craig, looking like a rose on a manure heap, was Liz Gaynor. She was crying.

"Tears will avail thee naught, girl," says Craig. "This earthly life is but a vale of tears. Only in the next world will thee know happiness. Seek it not on earth. It is a sinful fancy."

"I don't care what you say, I won't do it!" Liz cried. "And your son is a horrible man and ugly as the rest of you! You can't make me do it. And you can't keep watching me all the time. Sooner or later, I'll get my chance and get away from this rotten town!"

Josiah Craig got to his feet and walked over close to where Liz was sitting. "So thee finds the True Believers ugly, does thee?" he says. "Perhaps because I bear this mark, from the hand of God, thee would shun me and mine?" Craig pointed to the hideous purple lump on his face. "This mark," he says, "is the sign that God has given to the True Believers, as he has touched my wife, Charity. The mark serves to remind us in Celestial that this life we know is *meant* to be full of pain and suffering. How else would we know the true joys of Heaven?"

Then he puts his face real close to Liz's and says, "My sign will harm thee not, girl. Touch it!"

He grabs Liz's hand, and I could see her draw back, but Craig was too big and strong for her. He made her put her hand on that awful purple growth on his face. Liz gave a little cry, and I almost came through the window to help her. As I did, Liz spotted me. She gives another yelp.

It was lucky that when Liz seen me, the business with Craig's face was going on. Both Craig and his old lady was looking at Liz at the time she spotted me. They thought she was yelping because of having to touch Craig's face. I quick motioned to Liz to shut up and not let on she seen me. Man, she is one brave girl. She cooled it, and you'd of never known she had seen me through the window.

"It is of no import," Craig was saying to Liz. "Once thee has seen and spoken with the true God, thee will believe as we do. Thee will go to the grotto tomorrow night and be consecrated in our true faith."

"Amen, husband," says Craig's wife. At least it sounded something like that. It was the first I heard her talk. She had a cleft palate, I think.

"See the child to her bed, Charity," says Josiah Craig to his wife. "For the hour is late, and soon Jonathan will arrive from the grotto in the mine. Then, all will be prepared for tomorrow night."

Charity Craig went over to where Liz was sitting, like to help her up. But Liz pushed her away and got up by herself. Together, they went to the pantry room in back of the house. I seen a light go on, so I guess she lit a lamp.

Keeping close to the side of the house, I snuck around to the window where the light was burning. I was glad they was keeping her on a ground floor. There ain't any trees in the Craig yard, and I wouldn't of been able to get to a second floor bedroom without a ladder. True, it made it easier for her to break out, if she wanted to run for it. But like Karl said, where was she gonna run to?

In a few minutes, the lights in the house went out. Charity Craig locked the door to Liz's prison room and split for upstairs, where the bedrooms are in the house. I waited for I don't know how long. I wanted to make sure that everyone was asleep first. Then, I started scratching on the screen that covered the pantry room where Liz was locked up. I guess she didn't hear me. I scratched again and gave a dah-dah-dah-dah-dah——
—dah-dah knock against the window frame. But real soft.

In a second, I heard Liz's voice say, "Jimmy? Is that really you?"

"Yeah, it's me."

"Oh, thank heaven!" she says. "I thought I was losing my mind when I saw you at the window before. I thought you were a ghost!"

"Nah, I'm real, all right," I says. "I got thrown clear when the car hit. I was outa my head. I crawled out into the desert. A hermit found me and patched me up. I would of been here sooner, babe, but I was banged up real bad. I came to get you out of here."

"Oh, Jimmy," she says, starting to cry. "Mommy and Daddy are both dead!"

"I know, I know," I says. "But cool it, willya? If they

hear you, they might come down to find out what's going on."

"No, they won't," Liz says damply. "I've cried myself to sleep every night since I've been in this nightmare town. They don't pay any attention. I've run away twice and, each time, they brought me back. There's no place to run out there, Jimmy. Even if I knew where I was or running to . . ."

"It's okay, Liz," I says. "It'll be different this time. I got a map and a compass. We're gonna be all right. Now, let me get this screen off the window."

The full moonlight helped and, in a few, I had the window screen out of the frame. And when Liz got halfway through the window, I gave her my hand. I saw her real plain in the moonlight. Scared as she was, she was still the best-looking chick in the world to me. Then, I seen this awful look come over her face.

I whipped around just in time to see this dude that had come up behind me. He looks just like Josiah Craig, right down to the beard and blotch on his face. But he ain't got an apple-sized growth on his birthmark. Just as he punches me square in the face, I remember thinking, "This must be Jonathan Craig, the son that Karl and Josiah mentioned." Then that ham-like fist hit me, and I was out of it!

When I came to, I was tied to one of the straightback chairs in Craig's living room. I never wanted to see it from the inside, but there I was. They'd been giving me a way to go, Craig and his son. They wanted to know how I got there, and how come I know Liz Gaynor. They didn't make no connection between me and Karl Horstman. But I figured it was only a matter of time before they put two and two together.

They didn't make much of the stuff I was carrying when Jonathan Craig caught me outside of Liz's window. I didn't have the canteen, so I suppose that it fell nearby when Craig's son clouted me. But tomorrow, in the daylight, they'd for sure find it.

"I will ask thee again, boy," Craig was saying. "From whence did thee come? Who are thee?"

"I'm from Astoria in New York," I says. "And I told you my name a hundred times. I'm on vacation in the desert." I was trying to keep Horstman out of this for as long as I could, see?

"Lies!" Craig thunders. "Thee would not have known the girl, Elizabeth, nor where she was detained. Thee are not strangers to each other. Why else would she attempt to flee with thee, a complete stranger?"

"Maybe she likes my looks," I crack, meaning that the Craigs is one ugly bunch of mothers.

Craig didn't miss the joke, either. "Tempt me not to violence, boy," he growls. "Thee may revile me, but this I will endure and more, in the name of the Lord."

"Yeah?" I says, remembering my Bible readings, "Well, how about a little turn the other cheek with that moose over there?" I nodded my head toward Jonathan Craig. "Let me outa these ropes, and we'll see if he can do more than sucker punch a guy in the dark!"

" 'Vengeance is mine saith the Lord,' " quotes Josiah Craig. "If my son harmed thee, it is not meet for thee to seek revenge in kind. The Lord sees all and punishes all transgressors in time."

"Seems like a one-way street to me," I says. "This gorilla can knock me around and, some day, God's gonna make him sorry, huh?"

Craig crashes a huge paw down on the Bible that was standing on the pedestal. "Mock not the word of God, lest ye suffer the consequences!" he shouts.

"Seems to me that *you're* the ones mocking the word," I says, getting hot now. "You guys are like my uncle. You're all full of holy words. But when it comes to being good people, you don't even come close!" I reached for a word I heard Horstman use about the townies. "You're a bunch of hypocrites. If there was a God, He wouldn't let a bunch of monsters like you live!"

Craig whammed me one in the face so fast that it caught me by surprise. It tilted me back in my chair and made the room spin.

"Blasphemy!" he roars. "Thee is beyond redemption! Had thee but spoken the truth to my questions, I were prepared to offer thee a chance to join the True Church. I can see now that thee are the Devil's instrument."

"Ah, sit on it!" I says. Craig raised his hand, and I was getting ready for another shot in the chops. But he got control of himself and says, "We Celestians know how to deal with the minions of Satan! On Monday, after the Sabbath, we will punish thee as the Bible demands! Jonathan?" he says.

"Yes, father?" says the moose, getting up.

"Place this Devil's tool safely in the root cellar until we may judge and punish him," says Craig.

Jonathan Craig came over to my chair. He didn't even bother untying me. He picks me up, chair and all. And I weigh 175! He carried me clear out of the house and set me down near a cellar door. It's got a hasp on the outside but no lock. He opens the thing up and goes down a short flight of steps. In a second, he strikes a match and lights a kerosene lamp. Then he comes back and carries me, chair and all, into the middle of this room.

I looked around and seen that the place is full of potatoes, carrots, beets, and what have you, all in bins. The kerosene lamp is hanging from a beam in the ceiling. There I was in the middle of the room, far away from anything I could of used to get loose with. The floor under my chair ain't even a real floor. Just hard-packed dirt. The moose might be big, but he wasn't dumb. He didn't take no chances on me getting loose. Once he sets me down in the chair, he puts his big, ugly face close to mine and says, "Thee will wait here until judgment and punishment, vile tool of the Devil."

"Pretty neat," I says to the moose. "No trial, just 'judgment and punishment.' Must save you creeps a lotta time."

"Do not try my patience, blasphemer," says Jonathan Craig. "My father is a holy man. I am a less perfect instrument of God than he. I would snap thy vile neck, like a serpent's!"

I thought about the way Karl Horstman had snapped that rattler's neck. I couldn't help it; I got goose pimples. This dude was so big, he maybe could of done that to me! I was gonna give him a comeback answer, but just then he says, "Think and repent, blasphemer. Thy fate is sealed. On Monday, thee will meet thy master, Satan, in hell!"

There was no mistaking his meaning. These loons were gonna kill me on Monday, somehow! But I had to be sure of what he meant.

"Oh-ho!" I says. "You creeps don't mind a little bloodshed, so long as it ain't one of you, huh?"

"Creature of Darkness," Jonathan Craig says, "we would not soil our hands nor souls with thy vile blood. Thee will be put to death in the manner prescribed."

"Sure," I says. "You're gonna kill me with kindness, I bet."

"Nay," says the moose, missing my crack, "thee will be placed underneath a door which will be taken from its frame. Then, each in turn of the True Believers will place a heavy stone upon that door until the breath is crushed from thy evil body, and thy black soul returns to the pit and thy vile master, Satan!"

With this last piece of fun information, the moose blows out the lamp. I heard him put something through the hasp on the root cellar door from the outside. I knew he was still out there, and I wanted to holler something that'd really burn him, but all I could come up with was, "Up yours, creep!"

I don't know how long I was there in the dark. I know my hands went numb pretty soon. But finally, I fell asleep. It was a noise from outside that woke me up. I got ready to put up some kind of fight if this was going to be my last chance. Trouble was, I was tied up like a Thanksgiving turkey. All I could of done was maybe bite somebody.

When the door opened, I could see that I had slept through most of the day. The sun was almost down. But from being in the dark all that time, it was still bright enough to blind me. I could make out the figure of a big dude with a beard in silhouette.

"All right, you creep," I says. "Come and get me!"

"Will you shut up?" this voice says. "You'll get us both killed!"

I could of kissed him. It was Karl Horstman!

9 · The Grotto in the Mine

Karl came over to my chair. He must of had a knife, because I felt the ropes give way with a dry pop. Soon as I tried to stand up, I fell down. Then my hands started to hurt so bad, I couldn't believe it. Karl began rubbing my hands and feet.

"Ow" I yelp. "That hurts!"

"You'll hurt a lot more if we get caught," Karl whispers. "I have to get the circulation going in your extremities. We don't have much time. All the townies are in the church right now. In a little while, they're going to troop up to the lead mine and have a ceremony to induct Liz into their church."

"How are we gonna get her loose, then?" I says.

"We're not," Karl says. "She's in no immediate danger, as you are. You and I are going to set out for Martinsville soon as it's dark. We'll bring the authorities with us when we come back for your girl friend."

"How'd you know what happened?" I ask. "How'd you know I was here?"

Karl gives my feet an extra rub that felt like needles. "I was out painting this morning. I spotted some of the townies headed for my cabin. They trashed it when they didn't find me there. Trashed it and set it afire. They even took Rowena. I put it all together then. Figured you'd been caught, and my canteen had been found with you. By the way, thanks for that."

"Sorry," I says. "Craig's son sneaked up in the dark, and the sucker punched me while I was getting Liz out the window."

"Well, what's done is done," Karl says. "I also deduced that if you were a prisoner, you'd be at Craig's place. I searched the house soon as the townies all went into the church. I was almost ready to give up when I saw the peg set in the hasp of the root cellar door. I know that no one locks things in Celestial, so I guessed this was where you were. Can you walk now?"

I stood up and tried out my feet. I still hurt like crazy, but I could get around. "Yeah. Let's go," I said.

"Easy, easy," Karl says. "Let me check and make sure the services at the church are still going on."

He snuck up the stairs from the cellar and was gone for a few minutes. Then he stuck his head back in the door and whispers, "It's all clear. Let's get going!"

We circled the town and got back onto the trail up through the hills above Celestial. By the time we did, it was just about dark. The moon wasn't up yet. Then I seen what looked like a bunch of fireflies coming up the hillside. It was a procession of the townies carrying torches, and they was making for where we was!

"They're headed for the lead mine," Karl says. "Their holy of holies is in there, somehow. They'll have Liz with them, too."

I asked Karl if there wasn't some way we could maybe jump the townies that had Liz and get away into the hills. He shook his head. "Too risky," he says. "And if we get caught in the process, it's sure death for us, and no one will ever know that Liz is in Celestial. I know it's tough to do, Jimmy, but you *must* leave her here."

"But what if she won't join their church?" I ask. "Liz got a mind of her own. If she says something that sets them off, like I did, they could maybe even kill her, too!"

Karl sighed deeply. "Listen, Jimmy," he says, "if you're that concerned, we can take a chance on splitting up. I'll eavesdrop on their ceremony in the mine—if I can with relatively little danger. That way, when we take off, we'll know how urgent the circumstances are. Okay?"

"You got it," I says and stuck out my hand. Karl took it, and I all of a sudden realized that it was the first time Horstman ever touched me, except to doctor me. I didn't say nothing, though. It wasn't the time or place.

We watched the procession as it snaked up the hillside and finally disappeared, light by light, into the mine entrance. They didn't leave a guard outside. Then I seen why.

In a few minutes, about ten or twelve guys come out with torches. They split up in groups of three and started fanning out toward Karl's cabin.

"Search party," Karl whispers. "They don't know yet that you're gone. They're looking for me. Funny as it sounds, Jimmy, I think the safest place we both could be is the mine. It's the last place they'd think of to look."

Once the torches from the search party was out of sight, me and Karl headed for the mine. Along the way, I told him about how the Celestians was gonna do me in. With the door and rocks.

"They'd need another door for me," says Karl. "And when I go, it's going to be fighting, not like a pie crust. Rolled out flat."

"I'm with you, Karl," I says.

The moon was coming up now, and we could see the ground around the mine pretty clear. Karl motions me to stop any noise or talk, and we made it into the mine entrance. It was spooky inside, but not all that dark. Seems that as they went along, the townies left torches in holders on the shaft walls to light their path. We only had to follow the torches. Even without torches, we could have followed the sounds. The Celestians was having some kind of far-out services. You could hear them all the way to the mine entrance.

Karl kept poking his head into side branches off the main shaft.

"If anyone comes out unexpectedly," he whispers, "we need a place to duck into."

I'd never been in no mine before. But it looked just like they do in movies. It was an old-fashioned mine with rails for a cart running down the main way in. Following the tracks, the torches, and the sounds, we made a turn and almost walked in on the townies!

All of a sudden, the shaft opened into a great big room. Well, half room, half cave. It was about the size of a small movie house with a real high ceiling. And inside, it's all set up like a church. There was benches and, where the big room narrowed down to a small alcove, they had a pulpit, too.

The alcove was all decorated with funny signs. I mean, it was writing, but no kind of writing I ever seen before. Karl tells me under his breath that the writing is in Greek and Hebrew.

We was way in the back of the cavey-room, so I didn't see Liz at first. See, we could see Josiah Craig right off, on account of he was in the pulpit. But all we could see of the rest of the people there was their backs. Then I spotted Liz. She was the only woman in the place that wasn't wearing black. I guess her being the guest of honor at this ceremony, so to speak, made her different. She was dressed completely in white. The ceremony had been going on for a while. Josiah Craig was running his mouth from the pulpit.

"True Believers," he says, "we are met here tonight, in the holiest of holy shrines, to welcome a new member. Though she be not born among us, she has no kith nor kin. Long have I searched my conscience on the wisdom of taking an outsider into our fold. Yet, she is still comely and still pure by grace of her years. I could not allow her to return to the world of atheism and sin that lies outside Celestial."

"She wouldn't of been here at all if it wasn't for their roadblock," I whisper to Karl. Karl just motioned me to shut up.

Craig was still into his rap: "I have chosen this night for her induction into the True Believers," says Craig, "as it be the anniversary of the first time God appeared on this spot to my great-grandfather. It was then we True Believers were given the holy orders to establish this church."

One of the men from the crowd stood up. "Brother Craig," he says, "I would speak."

"Thee knows our custom, so speak freely," answers Craig.

"I would know then," says the guy, "how thee would accept an outsider, when the Word of God to Godfrey Craig was that we keep only to ourselves. And I have seen this girl. She has not the mark of the hand of God upon her."

"Oh-ho," whispers Horstman to me. "It seems that Josiah is bending the regulations. He wants Liz for his son but the rules are against it."

"I hear thee, Brother Williams," says Craig from the pulpit, "and much I thought about this decision. I took it as a sign, the way in which she was delivered to us. That her parents perished at our gate. It were a sign that although her sinful outsider parents were unworthy, the girl were still pure. As to the fact that she bears no marks, as true members of our faith, we must allow the word of God to a willing convert."

"Then let us hear from her own lips that she be a willing convert," says Williams.

"Here it comes," whispers Karl. "She'll renounce the conversion."

"Elizabeth Gaynor!" booms Craig from the pulpit. "Will thee embrace the faith of the True Believers? Stand and face those here assembled."

Liz got up like she was told. I seen from her face that she'd been crying. She looked dazed, like the day I seen her through the binoculars. I was ready to make my move when she told these loons to sit on it. I knew she wasn't gonna join their church. I nearly dropped through the floor when she says in a small, but clear voice, "I will accept the faith of the True Believers. Of my own free will."

"So be it!" Craig rumbles.

"So be it!" says everyone in the room.

"What's going on?" I whisper to Horstman. "Why did Liz say that?"

"I don't know," says Horstman. "Maybe she's been threatened. They might have said they'd put her to death with the both of us."

"Hear then the word of God!" hollers Craig from the pulpit. And he goes up to the alcove-altar space in the wall. He puts both his hands on the wall, on each side of the narrow alcove, and says, "Oh God of the

True Believers, will Thou speak to us?" Then it happened.

A section of the wall inside the alcove started to glow with a light so bright, I could hardly look at it. But it didn't bother Craig none. He turns around to the crowd, like it was him who made the light. "Behold thy God, each True Believer!" he shouts.

The light turns from white to red to green to finally a soft blue-green. Maybe it was that I had looked at the bright white too long. But it seemed to me that I could make out a shape in the blue-green light. It was like a man, but it wasn't. There was something wrong with the way the arms bent. And it looked to me like there was more than five fingers on each of the hands. And then, so help me, the *thing* inside the light spoke!

"I AM THE TRUE GOD OF THY FATHERS," it says. "WHAT WILL THEE HAVE OF ME?"

"Only Thy leave to love and adore Thee," says the whole crowd, like one person talking.

"AND WILL THEE KEEP ONLY TO ME?" says the shape.

"Only to Thee and eschew all others," says the crowd, like a bunch of parrots.

"AND HOW LONG SHALL THEE KEEP THY VIGIL, SPEAKING NOT OF MY PRESENCE HERE?"

"Until forever and ever and the return of God to the True Believers," they all say.

"This is pure ritual," whispers Karl to me. "They've

been giving these responses for years. They have to
have been. It's all pat and rehearsed!"

The shape in the blue light spoke again, "GO,
THEN, AND STAY NOT TOO LONG IN MY
PRESENCE. THE GOD OF THY FATHERS HAS
SPOKEN."

"Amen!" says the chorus of kooks.

"The sign has been given, the True Believers will
share the Kingdom of Heaven," hollers Craig.

"So shall it be!" they all say.

Then Josiah Craig spreads his arms out and says,
"Having heard the word of God and seen His glorious
form, I do declare this meeting ended."

The whole crowd gives another amen, then they all
file out. They moved so quick that they almost caught
me and Karl flat-footed. We quick ran to a turnoff in
the way out of the mine, the way we come in. I don't
mind telling you that my head was all jerked around.
Not just from Liz saying she'd join up, either. I mean,
what *was* that thing that talked to the loonies? It
couldn'ta really been God. But right then, me and Karl
was busy staying outa sight.

The drag was that when they left, they took the
torches in the shaft. By the time the last loon left,
carrying his torch, it was blacker than the cellar they
was keeping me in. Once Karl was sure they was all
gone, he lights a match. That's when I looked behind
me and nearly died. All the time we was hiding in the
turnoff, me and Karl was only about a foot away from a

big hole in the underground roadway. I took a look in the light of the match. The hole seemed to go straight down. If we'da moved another foot back, that woulda been it for us! I still had the shakes when me and Karl went back to the big room.

Karl lit some candles all around the room that the True Believers left behind. I sat down in one of the pews. I wanted to talk to Karl about why Liz said what she said. But he was all over the altar, looking at this, pushing at that. He was rapping, but I didn't know what he was talking about. I guess he was talking more to himself than to me.

"Incredible!" he says. "This shrine has to be a hundred years old. And this is the first I know about what really goes on here."

"I don't care about what goes on here," I says. "I wanna get outa here. We know Liz is safe for now, anyhow. Let's hit it for Martinsville, Karl."

"In a moment, Jimmy. In a moment," Karl says. "Now, where was Craig standing when the light came on?" He was feeling and pressing spots on the wall, back where the light showed before. "It's obviously something mechanical. Like a video tape or motion picture projection. But these people don't use electricity."

"Look, Karl," I says, "I don't care how the thing works. I just gotta get to the next town. I'll even go to the cops. I don't care what they do to me. I gotta know that Liz is gonna be okay."

"Jimmy, you're not using your head," says Karl impatiently. "These people obviously obey the directives of this device, whatever it is. If we know what it is, we can deal with them. I have a suspicion that Craig knows. It seems to be how he controls the others. And the Craigs have always been the high priests, I guess you'd call them, since the founding of their church."

"But they're making Liz join 'em," I says.

"She's a smart girl, that's all," says Karl, waving a hand. "She saw that you drew a death sentence for refusing their church. If she doesn't anger them, she can stay alive. And that's most of the battle, staying alive. Like Galileo did."

Now, I don't know anything about this Galileo dude. I don't have the education Karl does. But what he said made sense. As long as Liz didn't get these nut cases mad at her, at least they wouldn't harm her. But then I thought of Craig's big, ugly son. I was about to say something to Karl, but I never got the chance.

Karl was screwing around in the place where the bright light was before. I heard Karl say to himself, "Now, where was Craig standing?" He puts both his hands on the wall, like I saw Craig do at the ceremony. Nothing happens. Then Karl says, "Of course! A voice cue!" He puts his hands back on the same spots, and he says real loud, "Behold thy God, each True Believer!"

The bright light came on! Being closer than I was before, it almost blinded me. Like looking straight into the sun. Then this voice says, "I AM THE TRUE

GOD OF THY FATHERS. WHAT WILL THEE
HAVE OF ME?"

When the thing talked, I nearly plotzed. But it didn't
phase Karl none. All he did was laugh out loud and say,
"Some straight answers, sport." But the thing ran on.
"AND WILL THEE KEEP ONLY TO ME?" it says.

"It's a recording of some sort, all right," says Karl.
He was still fiddling around with the altar.

"AND HOW LONG SHALL THEE KEEP THY
VIGIL, SPEAKING NOT OF MY PRESENCE
HERE?" it says.

"Until I figure out how this light show works," says
Karl.

"GO, THEN, AND STAY NOT TOO LONG IN
MY PRESENCE. THE GOD OF THY FATHERS
HAS SPOKEN." I knew now what Karl meant. It
didn't matter what you said to the light thing. It still
said the same message. Like one of those telephone
answering gizmos.

Karl was rapping his knuckles against the wall of the
alcove. Then he goes to the pulpit. He took the big
Bible off its stand and put it on the pulpit. He took the
stand and started poking at the wall again. I asked him
what he was doing.

"The light is a hologram, Jimmy. A three-dimen-
sional projection of laser light. That's why it's bluish-
green in color. The power source has to be back here
somewhere. But this doesn't make sense. The True
Believers have been coming to this place for almost a
hundred years. And that was well before electric lights,

let alone lasers. There's no power source I know of that could last that long, granted the device is a hundred years old. And there's no power lines to the mine. There never have been. I think . . ."

Karl was still poking at the wall while he was talking to me. But he stopped all of a sudden. "Here it is!" he hollers. "This spot is hollow!" Then he really starts whamming away at the spot in the wall with the Bible stand. After a minute, he knocks off.

"No good," he says. "It's hollow, but it's too thick here. We need something better to dig with than this," he says, meaning the Bible stand. Then he takes a candle and tells me to stay put while he finds something to dig with. "There may be some old mining tools in a side shaft," he says.

I hate to sound chicken, but I was glad he wanted to go alone. I was thinking about that hole in the shaft we nearly fell into a little while back. While I was waiting, I had a chance to sit and think for the first time since I got caught by the moose outside of Craig's house. It didn't look good.

What really bugged me was why Liz said what she did. Oh, sure, Karl was probably right. Liz said it to stay alive. And she's a good enough actress to make it sound convincing. Then I thought about Jonathan Craig. He was probably licking his chops right now, thinking of how he was gonna be married to Liz. Right then, I wanted to get going for Martinsville. Karl could screw around with this light doo-hickey later on. When we come back with the cops.

It was like thinking about Horstman made him show up. He comes back into the room, real dirty. But he's got a pickax on his shoulder. "Found something to dig with," he says, like I didn't have eyes.

"Well, you dig, then," I says. "I'm splitting for Martinsville."

"Jimmy, Jimmy," says Karl, shaking his head. "Don't you realize what we've found here?"

"I don't know, and I don't care," I says. "I just know that the townies are gone, and we got a chance to get away. You can fool with this when we get back from Martinsville."

"Then consider this," Karl says. "We go to Martinsville and tell the authorities what's going on in Celestial. That town has been there for over a hundred years. And in all that time, not a speck of trouble with the Arizona authorities. Now, here we come, a semi-hermit and a kid wanted for interstate flight. Who will they believe? Us or the Celestians?"

"We can show them the wrecked car," I says.

"Can we?" says Karl. "Now that they figure we're already on our way to Martinsville, or at least I hope so, when they didn't find us out in the hills, all they have to do is bury the wreck in the sand and deny the whole thing. They could easily hide Liz in this place under guard until the authorities left."

"Well, jeez, Karl," I complained, "we gotta do *something*!"

"Exactly what I'm doing, lad," says Karl. "What

we've found here will have TV and newspaper report-
ers six deep. It's the find of the century!"

"What are you talking about?" I ask.

"Don't you see, Jimmy? Craig's word is law around
here because he knows how to operate the hologram
projector. If we unmask him as a false prophet, the
whole structure of Celestial will crumble. But that's not
the half of it! This device has been here for over a
hundred years!"

"So what?"

"How's your history, kid?" says Karl. "Our scientists
didn't discover the laser beam principle until about
twenty years ago. At the time the Celestians were first
worshiping here, there wasn't even electricity, let alone
a technology that could have developed a laser beam. I
think this device is extraterrestrial!"

10 · The Traveler of Space

"You gotta be kidding," I says. "Like in *Close Encounters*?"

"What?"

"*Close Encounters of the Third Kind,*" I says. "It's a flick. These aliens come down to earth in a flying saucer and . . ."

"Jimmy, I haven't seen a motion picture in nearly nine years," Karl says. "But so long as you grasp my meaning about extraterrestrial, it's okay with me. In any event, I believe the power source for this hologram is behind the alcove over there. If we can break through the wall where it sounds hollow, perhaps we can find it!"

Karl takes the pickax and goes over to the alcove. He takes a great swing and starts in digging. I got up from where I was sitting and went over to him. "Wanna take turns digging?" I ask. He grins, nods, and keeps swinging the pickax.

It took us maybe three hours to break through the

wall. Good thing it didn't take too much longer. The candles that the townies left behind was running low. The breakthrough happened while I was digging. For once, the rock didn't chip off. The point of the ax stuck in the rock, like when you drive a nail into a hollow wall.

After that, it went faster. Inside a half hour, we made the hole in the alcove big enough to squeeze through. Karl was trying to see into the dark with the candle, but soon as he stuck his head and the candle through the hole to have a look-see, the candle blew out.

"A draft," says Karl. "That means there's another way out besides this hole. If there's air coming through enough to blow out the candle, there's an exit, or at least an air shaft, someplace inside! Jimmy, go back to the shaft entrance. Get one of those shielded candle holders, the mining lamps, from a wall niche. I'll make the hole bigger while you're gone."

I done like Karl asked and, by the time I got back, he had the hole in the wall big enough for us to walk through if you bent over a little. The mining lamp kept the light burning. There was a room just as big as the cave room on the other side of the alcove! We walked real careful, on accounta there coulda been another shaft, like outside. But when Karl held the candle up over his head, and our eyes got used to the dark, we could see that there wasn't no holes in the floor. And that wasn't all we could see.

All right, here it comes. You can believe me or not.

Most of the big room was filled up with this huge, far-out looking machine! It was so big, at first, I thought it was something like a piece of mining equipment. Don't ask me why I thought that. I wouldna known what mining equipment looked like. I never seen none before. But I figure if you're in a mine and you find a great big hunk of machine, it's gotta be something they use in a mine, right? But that was because in the candlelight, you could only see a little bit of it at a time. Karl was fiddling around the thing and rapping away like Arnie Skaggs with a skinful of speed.

"Look at it!" he hollers. "Just look at it! I had my suspicions before. The lines in the desert where I hunt. No one knows how they got there or why. The designs they form from the air—they all pointed this way, and I was too stupid or wrapped up in my own problems to see it! Incredible! Maybe Von Daniken was right after all!"

I didn't have no idea what he was talking about. "Look, man," I says. "I dunno what you're carrying on about or how it's gonna help us any. All I see is this big piece of machinery. I got no more idea what it's about than the man in the moon." And when I says this, Karl busts out laughing, like a crazy man. "Not the man in the moon, Jimmy. The man from the stars!" and he starts laughing again.

"Have you flipped?" I says. But it's like I didn't say nothing. Horstman is almost jumping up and down, and he's grinning and laughing.

"No, I haven't," he says. "All I've done is make the greatest scientific find of our age. Of any age. In all history! Can't you see?" Horstman crows. "This is a space craft of some sort. But I don't see an entrance or an opening in the hull. I wonder how you get inside?" And with this, he's off running his hands all over the thing. Maybe feeling for a doorknob, if there's such things on a UFO. I went with him this time.

It was big, all right. I figure it was easy thirty feet high, at the top, and easy fifty-five feet long. It wasn't no saucer shape, either. Once we walked around it a coupla times, we could tell it was shaped more like a oval bar of soap with a big hump in the middle. The metal it was made out of was smooth as glass. You couldn't find a lumpy spot or even a rough spot any place on it. And the funny thing about it, the metal wasn't cold to the touch. It wasn't warm either. Just maybe lukewarm.

We musta scrambled over the thing for an hour, but we couldn't find no way to get inside. Not that I wanted to. Karl did. Even he finally gives up.

"We'll have to come back with work lights and a crew," he says. "I can't make any more progress without adequate light. But this just may be enough to show the townies." Karl laughed that unfunny laugh of his. "Here's their True God, Jimmy. What they were ready to kill you and me for. What a collection of superstitious semi-savages these men are, Jim. What they couldn't understand, they fell down and worshiped."

Karl was futzing around with a standing piece of machinery near to the alcove entrance when it happened. All of a sudden, it was bright as daylight in the room! I could see the machine real clear. Karl was standing at the other machine near the alcove, a look of wonder on his face. He turned around and fiddled some more with the panel on the machine, and a section of the big oval . . . spaceship, I guess you'd have to call it, slides open!

There was this bluish light inside the ship, and I could see passageways leading off the part we could see from outside. I don't mind saying I was scared. Maybe all those science fiction flicks I saw when I was little came to my mind. But Karl ain't scared at all. He almost runs up the ramp that slid out of the spaceship. He waves to me and says, "Coming?" I wasn't too hot for it but I went in, too.

We found its body in the control cabin. I don't know how long the thing had been there. It was almost human looking. And somehow, it looked familiar to me. Then I realized that this alien-thing was what we all saw in the laser projection outside in the shrine the townies built. I didn't want to go near it, but Karl touched it. Brrr! I backed away and bumped into something, I don't know what. The walls of the control cabin were covered with funny-looking dials and switches. All in a language and figures I couldn't make sense of. So I couldn't tell you which one I touched to set the thing off.

"Welcome and be joyous," says this voice. "Long have I waited. Your deliverance comes too late. I have terminated."

"What the . . . ?" I said.

Karl motioned me to shut up. We both sat back and listened while the voice ran on. "After having completed routine cultural profile of this planet, which at this recording is a Stage III, I developed leakage from the drive-shielding of my ship. Realizing that I had to make repairs, I selected this site. It is a crude form of mineral-rendering that the inhabitants of this planet practice. They actually excavate, remove the minerals in a raw state, and purify at another site. However, the mineral content of this location is rich in a substance which can provide adequate new shielding, granted I can make the necessary repairs."

I nudged Karl. But he shushed me again. The thing went on. "Unfortunately, after making proper guide signals visible from orbit above the planet, and after preparing an adequate work space for repairs, my site was discovered by the local inhabitants. Knowing the injunction against contact with primitive cultures, I installed a projector. I used a message understandable to their mentalities and warned them away. I played on their local superstitions. The purpose was twofold. First, it gave me the privacy I required for repairs and, second, the inhabitants are quite fragile physically. Even small amounts of energy do them great harm.

"It was then," the voice went on, "I discovered that

the energy-concentrator nozzle was fused. I set my distress beacon and, to conserve rations, decreased my life functions to maintenance level. I estimate I can remain functioning for another seventy-five revolutions of this planet about its sun. They who find this recording will therefore know that I have served the Union of Cultures to the best of my abilities. I would suggest that the nozzle design of the drive unit be revised to prevent this from befalling another cultural survey ship. I send regards of deepest respect to the Union Council, and my regrets to my surviving clan members that I shall never know their presence again. So, farewell and be joyous!" Then the message stopped.

We sat there for a few minutes, not saying a word. Karl talked first. "Telepathic projection," he says.

"Huh?"

"Didn't it strike you odd that we understood everything, Jimmy?" says Horstman. "Surely, this alien didn't speak our language. And the message wasn't left for human ears to hear. The message was recorded on a telepathic machine of some sort. It explains why we didn't find any external speakers to go with that hologram projector outside. It works directly on the mind itself!"

"I guess I understand," I said, "but we really ought to . . ."

"Oh, no!" says Karl, slapping his forehead. "Let's get out of here, Jimmy, and fast!"

"What's wrong?" I ask.

"Radiation!" Karl says. "That laser hologram was a KEEP OUT sign. And that's why the townies are so bent and twisted! They've been coming up here once a week for almost a hundred years, to worship." Karl laughed bitterly. "Their True God has been systematically warping their genetic makeup with hard radiation for years! And being isolated and intermarrying, they've turned themselves into the freaks and monsters they are today. Those fools, those stupid fools!" Karl moved to the entrance hole we dug, and he waves me to follow.

We walked down the main shaft toward the entrance, Karl rapping all the way. "Don't you get it, Jimmy? I wondered how long something like this could go undiscovered, but it makes sense. Being in a lead mine, the radioactivity wouldn't be detectable. Not even to a flyover satellite on a radiation survey. Evidently, the alien was used to a much higher level of radiation than humans. And the hologram was intended to keep the townies away. Remember, it said, 'Stay not too long in my presence?' The alien left it running while he was waiting for a rescue craft. He died still waiting. But the keep-away device went on working. The alien didn't know as much about human psychology as it thought it did. Tell a lunatic fringe religious person to stay away, and it's the biggest come-on in the universe!"

We got out of the mine and carefully scouted the area for any sign of townies. They would of been easy to spot. With them carrying torches, you could spot them a distance away. Karl was still high on what we found. Maybe for him a big thing, all the technical stuff. But in my mind, all I could see was that thing with the funny joints, instead of elbows and knees, and six fingers on each hand. Even inside its space suit, it looked creepy. I made up my mind that no matter what happened, I wasn't going back into that room with the ship in it.

"This is marvelous, Jimmy," Karl kept saying. "With a find like this, they'll have to take us seriously in Martinsville. We don't have to explain to the local police. We can call the Federal Government. They have agencies that investigate such things."

Swell, I think, but this ain't getting us going. And it's getting later and later. Like Karl said, we hadda cross the desert before the sun came up. I mentioned it to him. He just waved a hand. "Listen, Jimmy, even if we're caught by the townies, all I have to do is get them to take a look for themselves. They can't deny this, even to themselves!"

"What if they don't give us no chance to explain?" I says. "You know, they do us up on the spot, they find us, and that's it!"

"You may be right, Jimmy," he says. "There's no point in taking any chances."

The moon was almost down now, and it was getting dark on the hillside. It got tricky seeing where we was going without no light. And we wasn't about to take a chance and strike a light. It'd be visible for miles in the desert. I was just thinking that, when I missed my footing and fell. I slid partway down the hill and come up against a rock ledge about ten yards down. But when I tried to get up, I couldn't. My foot was wedged between a big flat rock and the hillside.

Karl got down to where I was stuck, and I told him what was the matter. "Oh, no," he says. "There isn't a stick or a tree on this hill that I could use to pry you loose, Jimmy." Then he starts feeling around the rock where my foot is stuck. "Maybe I can get your foot free if I could only see. Jimmy, I'm going to have to take a chance on striking a match. But if there's a search party in the hills, they're bound to spot it now that the moonlight is failing."

"Do what you gotta do," I says.

"All right," he says, "but if we're spotted, and I still can't get you loose . . ."

"Then you leave me here and hustle your buns to Martinsville," I says. "If I'm stuck, I'm stuck. All I gotta do is tell 'em what's up there in the mine, like you said. At least it'll buy you some time to make the run to Martinsville."

Karl lit the match. "Not too bad," he says. "I think that if you can get your sneaker off, you can wiggle your foot free. I'll cut the laces." Karl took out his jackknife. "I'll have to strike another match," he says.

"Okay, okay," I says. "But hurry up!" Just when Karl lit the second match, I saw them. A bunch of lanterns like a string of Christmas tree lights moving up the hillside. They must of been searching in the dark and, when they seen our light, they had us.

I felt the laces in my sneaker part when Karl cut them. I wiggled my foot like crazy and, even though I scraped my ankle pretty bad, my foot came loose! I felt my sneaker fall off and go sliding further under the big rock. I stood up, and my foot felt okay. I pointed out the lights coming toward us to Karl and said, "We been seen. Let's get going!"

"Just a second," Karl says. "I have to get your sneaker out from under there. The ground is sharp here, and there's cactus. You're going to need that sneaker if we're going to make any kind of run for it."

I heard him scrambling around under the rock, reaching. And then I heard that sound. I heard it before, and it's one you never forget. Almost at the same time, I heard Karl cry out, "Rattlesnake! It got me!"

11 · The Desert in the Daylight

"Get out of here," Karl says. "Here's your sneaker. Get going!"

"Not without you, Karl," I says. "We been spotted, and they're coming up the hill. I can see them!"

"I can't go anywhere until I take care of this bite," says Karl. "Any activity makes the poison get into the bloodstream faster. I have to cut the wound and put a tourniquet on it."

He was working real fast with the jackknife in his good hand. He already had his belt off and twisted around his upper arm. He was sucking out the blood and spitting it on the ground.

"Listen, Jimmy," he says. "You were ready to stay here and stall the townies so that I could get away. I'm doing the same thing for you. I couldn't get far this way, anyhow. I just delivered some serum to the Craig house. It's my only hope. I *have* to deal with the townies. And if I can get them talking, they just might go up to the mine to see for themselves what we've found. Do you still have your pocket compass?"

"Yeah," I says. "The map, too. They didn't take them away."

"Good," he says. "There's an outside chance they don't know you're still not in the root cellar. They may be satisfied with capturing me. They might stop the search. Now get going!"

"Okay, okay," I says. I got my sneaker on, no laces and all. I ran about twenty feet, then I stopped. I looked back at Karl, laying there on the ground. I couldn't see his face too good. I called back, "I'll see you soon, Karl. And . . ."

"Yes, yes," says Karl, "what is it?"

"I just wanted to say thanks."

"Will you get out of here?" he hollers. I ran about a hundred yards when I heard him call out, "You're welcome, Jimmy." It put some steam in my running when he said that.

I was easy a quarter of a mile away when I seen the lights reach where Karl was. It was like a bunch of fireflies swarming into one spot. After that, I didn't look back but once. And that was almost a couple of hours later.

I was maybe a few miles away, or I figure it was that far. I heard you can walk a mile in about fifteen minutes. I had been running, then jogging for a long time. It could of been maybe five miles. But I finally hadda slow down, on account of there was no more moonlight. Anyhow, all of a sudden, the whole desert lights up like it was broad daylight!

I turned around in time to see a great, big fireball and a light so intense I couldn't believe it. It looked like an atom bomb explosion but a lot smaller. The light was so bright that when I looked away from the thing, I couldn't see at all. Then I heard the noise. The whole ground shook where I was standing. I watched the cloud turn from white to red, then purple with red sparkles in it.

When I turn around, I'm blind. I mean, like a bat. I put my hand up in front of my face, and all I can see is that purple cloud with red sparks in it. I tried to keep going, but I tripped and fell down. No getting away from it. I was for sure blind. I was dog tired, my foot hurt where I scraped it, my shoulder was starting to hurt all over again. Wouldn'tcha know when I tripped, I landed on my bad shoulder? I knew when I was whipped. I fell down on the sand, and I . . . well, I cried, man. I cried like I never cried since my mom died. I guess after a while, I went to sleep.

When I woke up, I was dreaming that I died and went to Hell. I was burning up, and Josiah Craig was the Devil, jabbing me with his pitchfork in the shoulder. But once I opened my eyes, I discovered I could see! It was bright daylight, and what I thought was the fires of Hell was only the Arizona sun on the desert. I still couldn't see too good. Anytime I closed my eyes, I could still see that purple cloud with red sparkles. And even with my eyes open, I could see it like a ghost image.

Then all of a sudden, it dawned on me. I was in more trouble out here than back in Celestial. I had a bum foot, I was half blind, the sun was up, and I didn't have drop one of water!

I got my wool shirt up over my head to keep the sun off, and I started walking. I followed the compass directions like Karl said to do. But man, talk about miles and miles of nothing. I sure hoped the compass was working okay. Because you get out there, you can't see anything. You could walk in a circle and never know, on accounta everything looks the same. You could maybe walk by the same spot a hundred times and not know. It looks just like every other spot in that place.

Two hours later, I figure by the sun, I fell down for the first time. Weird feeling, man. It's like you're walking along, and, yeah, you feel hot and tired and real thirsty. No words to say how thirsty. At first, you sweat. Then you got no more water left in your body to sweat with. After that, you can't even wet your lips with your tongue, and you start getting blisters and sores on your lips.

Then you start getting dizzy and hallucinating, like behind acid. Man, I saw some of the weirdest things out there. I even seen my mom. She was standing about a hundred yards away and waving to me. But the way she was waving to me wasn't the way the compass told me to go. I kept walking, then she starts crying. Now, I knew it couldn't really be her. But you get so punchy after a while, nothing makes sense, and nothing that's real is real anymore, if you dig what I'm saying. Then it was like all my arms and legs was made outa straw. A hot wind came up, and it blew me down to the sand. Like I didn't have no weight at all. I don't know how long I stayed down. I don't remember even getting up again, but I musta.

The second time I fell down, I knew it was over for me. No way I could get up again. That's when I seen the highway. I'd been seeing the highway on and off since the sun come up. But I knew it couldn't be the highway, on accounta Karl's compass. I figured I was going crazy from the heat and no water, so I kept on hiking.

This time when I seen the highway, it was different. Before, all I seen was the road itself. But this time, I seen cars. I even seen a truck go by. I tried to holler out, but I was too far away. Then I realized it was another hallucination. Cars or not. I mean, didn't I see my mother before, just as clear? To show you how gonezo I was, I seen this car stop on the roadside and a dude in a summer suit and a hat and shades get out. He had this camera, and he was taking shots of the desert. Which right away told me this was another bad dream. Ain't nothing out there to take pictures of, I mean.

All of a sudden, the whole thing struck me funny. I break out laughing. I somehow get to my feet. I was gonna holler at this dude and tell him how funny he looked, taking pictures of nothing. I tried to holler but nothing comes out. Then he sees me and waves. I throw him a finger, and I fall down again.

I figured when I came to, I was already dead and in Heaven. On accounta it was air-conditioned. But I was in a bed. And every time I moved, something somewhere hurt me. I was, like, all wrapped up in some kinda plastic with gooey crap all over me. Then the nurse comes in and says, "Oh. Back with us, I see." She comes over and takes my pulse and sticks a thermometer in my mouth. And, naturally, knowing I can't talk with it in my mouth, she starts rapping at me.

"You gave us quite a fright, young man," she says. "For a while there, we thought we were going to lose you. Second degree sunburn, dehydration, heat exhaustion, scrapes, bruises, a partly healed fracture of the collarbone. You were a mess!"

Just then a doctor comes in. He went right over to the bed and takes the thermometer outa my mouth and checks it. I wanted to say, "Call the cops. I got some friends in danger." But all that came out was a dry, creaky sound.

"Don't try to talk, young man," he says. "You're in Sunland General Hospital in Martinsville. You were found near the interstate, nearly dead. I'd stop and chat with you, but your vocal chords, like the rest of your body, aren't working too well. In any event, you'll be all right in a few days. Right now, I have a full-fledged disaster to contend with. I have patients in the burn ward stacked like cordwood." He told the nurse to bring something that turned out to be a needle, which he slips into my arm. After that, I went out. I guess it was like the Demerol Karl give me. I spun out the same way.

It was a coupla days before anybody would stop long enough to pay any attention to me. I knew something big was going on, the way that every time I came around from the dope they kept shooting me with, no one would stop and talk with me. It was driving me bats. For all I knew, those coo-coos had crushed Karl Horstman under a door by now. And Liz . . . well, she coulda been married off to the moose. And I couldn't make anybody stop and listen to what I had to say. The one time I tried to get outa bed to find somebody, they slipped me another shot, and I was out again. It was the nurse I seen the first time I woke up who finally filled me in on what happened.

She come bopping in, real cheery. And when she seen I was awake, she says, "How are we feeling today? Pain better?"

"Yeah," I says. "But I got to talk to some cops. There's something happening."

"Don't you worry about the police, Mr. Hunter . . . isn't it?"

"Howdja know my name?" I ask.

"It's right here on your chart," she says, smiling. "You had some I.D. in your wallet when you were found. We turned it over to the police as a matter of routine. If things hadn't been so hectic around here, you'd be our number one mystery patient. The staff was talking about you. Wandering in the desert, no automobile, I.D. from New York City. And the police *do* want a word with you. I was told that when you're able to have visitors, the police are the first who want to talk to you."

"I bet they do," I says. "But I gotta talk to them right away. I got some friends that are in worse trouble. They're back in Celestial."

"Oh!" she says, like that explains everything. "You're one of the Celestial survivors!"

"Whadda you mean, survivors?" I yelp. "What happened?"

"You're probably the only person in the United States who doesn't know," she says. "There was an atomic blast in Celestial three days ago. We were swamped with victims. Everyone says that an Air Force plane with a nuclear warhead aboard must have crashed just outside of Celestial. There were many killed. And of the survivors, a lot of them have radiation poisoning. Poor creatures. Not only are they deformed from birth, but to have this happen to them. It doesn't seem fair, somehow. Then, talk about busy! We were going around the clock here for forty-eight hours!"

My heart felt like a lump of lead in my chest. Liz . . . Karl. Both of them most likely dead or dying. And now, the cops waiting to take me back to dear, sweet Uncle Andy. Maybe even jail. I wanted to die right then.

"Are you in pain?" asked the nurse.

I didn't wanna explain, so I just said yeah. She slips me another shot, and I slept some more. When I wake up, I feel somebody's taking my pulse again. I open my eyes, and I'm looking straight into Karl Horstman's face. I almost didn't know it was him. He had a big bandage that covered the left side of his face. And I guess to get the bandages on him, they hadda shave off his beard and cut his hair. But there wasn't no mistake about his eyes. He was sitting in a wheelchair, alongside my bed.

"How do you feel, Jimmy?" he says.

"Liz?" I says right off.

"In the hospital at Winslow. They have a bigger facility for burns there. But I checked. She's in rough shape, but she's going to make it.

"What happened?" I asked Karl. "The nurse said a Air Force plane with a bomb on it hit Celestial. I seen the blast and didn't know what it was. I was maybe five miles away. What a freaky accident to happen!"

"It wasn't an Air Force plane, Jimmy," Karl says. "It was the spacecraft in the mine that blew. It took off half the hilltop. The only reason that either of us is still here is that it took place in a lead mine, which shielded most of Celestial from the main part of the blast."

"But how?"

"If I knew the answer to that one, I wouldn't be here," Karl says. "The snake bite wasn't as bad as I thought it was. I got the biggest part of the venom out by acting quickly. Maybe the rattler wasn't a big one.

The Celestians were about to throw me in the root cellar when they discovered you were gone. I tried to stall for time. I told them about what we'd found in the mine. I accused the Craigs of hoaxing the town for generations. Not true, of course. The Craigs really believed that God was in the mine. But I stirred up enough controversy to make a group take a look up there."

"Then how'd the thing blow up?" I asked.

"That, I couldn't say," Karl answers. "I was in no shape to go with them. Both the Craigs and some other men in authority went up there to have a look. My guess is that Josiah took one look and denounced it as the Devil's work. He could have taken the pickax to some of the machinery. Or maybe just touched a switch he shouldn't have. We'll never know."

"But Liz didn't go with them?"

"No, they left her at the Craig house, under guard. When the spaceship blew, she was upstairs. That's why she was so badly burned. I was in the root cellar and protected. I got hit by a falling timber. That's how I got this," he says, pointing to his bandage.

"But, Liz," I said. "Is she gonna be all right?"

Karl avoided my eyes, and I knew something was wrong. He cleared his throat and said, "Uh, sure she will, Jimmy. I've spoken with her. And you might be interested to know why she went along with joining the church that night in the mine. It seems Jonathan Craig told her that if she joined, he'd try to get your life spared."

"Why that dirty . . ."

"Now, now," says Karl, waving a finger. "Let's not speak ill of the dead."

"No big loss," I says. "But how soon can I see Liz?"

"A touchy question, Jimmy," Karl says. "You first must see the local police. When that reporter found you near the roadside, all your I.D. was turned over to the police. They called New York City and got the score on you from your uncle."

"Oh, swell."

"It's not as bad as you might think, Jimmy," Karl says. "I've spoken with the police here. Your Uncle Andy didn't press any criminal charges against you. He just reported to the police that you'd run away. Said you were failing in school, that's why you ran away."

"He lies!" I says.

"Naturally," Karl says. "Would he tell the truth and admit he'd been beating you? Funny thing, Jimmy. You just never understood your rights in that custody situation with your uncle. If the first time he beat you, you'd have gone to the court, you'd have been out of your uncle's house years ago."

"I just didn't know."

"And he wasn't about to tell you. He got money from the state for your support. Did you know that, either?"

"Nope," I says. "I guess I was pretty dumb, huh?"

"No, Jimmy," Karl says, smiling. "You were young, hurt, and defenseless. There was no reason for you to know about the courts for redress. When you were hurt, you struck back. Out of fear and pain. If there's to be a hearing on this in New York, I'll be with you."

"You?" I ask. "What for? I thought soon as you got better, you'd be back out there in the desert building a new place."

"It's all ashes now, Jimmy, in more ways than one," Karl says. "It took something like this to make me realize what a fool I'd been for eight years. You can't shut out the world; resign your membership in the human race. Look what that did to the people of Celestial."

"When can I see Liz?"

"I'm not your doctor, Jimmy. I'd say from the shape you're in, you could see her in a few days. But she won't see you. I know. I spoke to her on the phone today."

"Whadda you mean, she won't see me?" I holler. "Why not?"

"She's been badly burned about the face and neck, Jimmy," Karl says. "And she's also lost the vision in her right eye. She's been disfigured, and she doesn't want anyone to see her. Least of all you."

"That's crazy!" I hollered. "What do I care? She's still Liz, ain't she? I don't care what she looks like. I . . . I love her!"

I never seen Karl Horstman smile so big before or since.

"Well said, lad!" he says. "You didn't even ask about plastic surgery for repair of her burns. Ready to take her any way at all. You may have had an unfortunate upbringing, son, but there's no doubt you're a gentleman of some class." He picked up the phone by my bedside and handed it to me. "The number is WInslow 5-6200. She's in room 214. Just ask the hospital operator to put you through." Before I could grab the telephone, he took it outa my reach and says, "She still doesn't want to see you until the burns are healed, and she can have the corrective surgery done. I told her I had an idea you wouldn't want to wait a year or so."

"A year or so?" I hollered. "I'm going to Winslow tomorrow!"

The hospital operator in Winslow didn't want to put me through to Liz. Karl had to get on the phone. "This is Dr. Horstman," he says. "I'm consulting there with Dr. Kramer. Put this call through to 214 or I'll have your job, do you understand?" Then he winks and hands me the phone. "Sometimes you have to throw your weight around," he says. Then Liz came on the line.

"Hello?"

"Hi, Liz. It's me, Jimmy."

"Hello, Jimmy."

"Hello? That's it?" I says. "Nothing else?"

"I'm . . . not feeling too well today, Jimmy," she says.

"Listen, Liz," I says. "Ain't no need to lie to me or to be cool. Karl Horstman is right here with me. He already told me what happened to you. And, Liz, it doesn't matter to me. Do you hear? Baby, you still there? "

"Yes . . ."

"I love you, Liz. I want to see you as soon as I can!"

I looked over at Karl, and he gives me a big grin and makes an okay sign with his thumb and fingers. Then he wheels himself out of the room, real quiet. I appreciated that. After all, me and Liz had a lot to talk about.